MW00526896

MURDER BUYS A ONE-WAY TICKET

Books by Laura Levine

THIS PEN FOR HIRE
LAST WRITES
KILLER BLONDE
SHOES TO DIE FOR
THE PMS MURDER
DEATH BY PANTYHOSE
CANDY CANE MURDER
KILLING BRIDEZILLA
KILLER CRUISE
DEATH OF A TROPHY WIFE
GINGERBREAD COOKIE MURDER
PAMPERED TO DEATH
DEATH OF A NEIGHBORHOOD WITCH
KILLING CUPID
DEATH BY TIARA
MURDER HAS NINE LIVES
DEATH OF A BACHELORETTE
DEATH OF A NEIGHBORHOOD SCROOGE
DEATH OF A GIGOLO
CHRISTMAS SWEETS
MURDER GETS A MAKEOVER
DEATH BY SMOOTHIE
MURDER BUYS A ONE-WAY TICKET

Published by Kensington Publishing Corp.

MURDER BUYS A ONE-WAY TICKET

LAURA LEVINE

Kensington Publishing Corp.
www.kensingtonbooks.com

KENSINGTON BOOKS are published by

Kensington Publishing Corp.
900 Third Avenue
New York, NY 10022

All Kensington Titles, Imprints, and Distributed Lines are available at special quantity discounts for bulk purchases for sales promotions, premiums, fund-raising, and educational or institutional use. Special book excerpts or customized printings can also be created to fit specific needs. For details, write or phone the office of the Kensington special sales manager: Kensington Publishing Corp., 900 Third Ave., New York, NY 10022, attn: Special Sales Department, Phone: 1-800-221-2647.

Library of Congress Control Number: 2024932400

KENSINGTON and the KENSINGTON COZIES teapot logo Reg. US Pat. & TM Off.

ISBN: 978-1-4967-2819-7

First Kensington Hardcover Edition: July 2024

ISBN: 978-1-4967-2821-0 (ebook)

10 9 8 7 6 5 4 3 2 1

Printed in the United States of America

For my readers, with love and gratitude.

ACKNOWLEDGMENTS

Heartfelt thanks to John Scognamiglio, for taking a chance on Jaine twenty-two years ago, and who has been an absolute dream of an editor ever since. To Evan Marshall, who got the ball rolling, for his wise counsel and expert hand-holding. To Hiro Kimura, whose cover art never fails to delight me. To Lou Malcangi, for his eye-catching dustjacket designs. And the rest of the gang at Kensington who keep Jaine and Prozac coming back for murder and minced mackerel guts.

To Versel Rush, for her generous bid in Kensington's Ukrainian relief auction. (And for knitting me the most adorable beanie, scarf, and booties.) It was such a kick naming a character after you!

To my grandniece Denin Levine Grundvig, an Amtrak engineer—yes, my sweetie pie grandniece actually drives those ginormous trains—for providing me with so many valuable facts about train travel, more than a few of which I'm afraid I've mangled.

To Dorothy Howell, multi-talented author of the Sewing Studio and Haley Randolph Mysteries, who's bailed me out of many a plot hole.

To Joanne Fluke and Mark Baker. To Mara and Lisa Lideks. And to my friends and family for your love and encouragement.

Finally, a loving thank you to my readers for hanging in there with me all these years. Your sweet notes and posts have brought much joy to my life. I'm grateful for every single one of you.

Chapter One

Some people sculpt their bodies into shape with Pilates. Others burn off unwanted calories in spin class. Still others run miles each day on the treadmill.

Don't you just hate those people? As for me, whenever I feel like I should be exercising, I lie down until the feeling goes away.

Which is why I was surprised (shocked, really) to land a job ghostwriting a fitness guidebook.

It all started when I answered an online ad for a nonfiction writer. I'd almost forgotten I'd even applied for the job when, weeks later, I got an email from Chip Miller, owner of The Muscle Factory, a nationwide chain of gyms, asking me to come in for an interview.

My heart sank when I realized I'd be meeting up with a fitness guru, certain he'd take one look at my muscle-free bod and send me packing. But a job was a job, and I couldn't afford to pass up an opportunity to earn some much-needed dinero.

So on the morning in question, after polishing off a cinnamon raisin bagel, slathered with butter and strawberry jam, I donned my go-to job interview outfit (skinny jeans, silk blouse, and blazer) and headed out into the living room.

"How do I look?" I asked my cat, Prozac, who was hard at work on the sofa, attacking an evil throw pillow from Planet Chenille.

She paused in her attack to shoot me a withering glare.

Like someone who should be staying home and giving her beloved cat a belly rub instead of traipsing off to a job interview.

If only I'd paid attention to her.

Instead, I grabbed my car keys and was soon tooling off in my ancient Corolla to meet up with Chip Miller at his McMansion in Bel Air—a palatial affair with towers and turrets and more wings than a flock of geese.

Think Windsor Castle with palm trees.

After parking my car in front of a six-car garage, I sucked in my gut and trekked over to an imposing front door with the initials "CM" carved into the woodwork. I rang the bell, setting off a series of cathedral-like chimes and, seconds later, was greeted by a rosy-cheeked maid in a floral apron who led me down a maze of corridors to Chip's office.

Everything about the office seemed designed to intimidate: the massive desk, the hotel lobby–sized sofa and armchairs, the walls plastered with celebrity photos, and the boatload of trophies on display in a glass-enclosed case.

Dominating the scene was Chip Miller himself, a spray-tanned, sixtysomething guy in shorts and a tank top, running on a treadmill as he barked orders to some hapless soul at the other end of his Bluetooth.

"If enrollment isn't up five percent next month, you're history. I don't care if you just had open-heart surgery. Get off your lazy butt and start hustling."

"Jaine Austen here to see you," said the maid when he'd finished his harangue.

Chip looked me up and down, not exactly radiating approval. I was all set to be summarily banished with a disparaging comment about my childbearing hips when he asked, "Want a wheatgrass smoothie?"

Yuck, no. If God had meant grass to be pureed in a blender, He'd have never invented the strawberry daiquiri.

"Sounds tempting, but I'll pass."

After dismissing his maid, Chip waved me to a seat, all the while pounding away on his treadmill.

I was getting exhausted just looking at him.

"Here's the deal, sweetheart."

Sweetheart? Under what feminist-free rock had this guy been hiding for the last decade?

"I need someone to help me write a fitness book."

Just as I'd feared. Talk about being unqualified for the job. But in the interests of scoring a paycheck, I plastered on an enthusiastic smile.

"Sounds intriguing, Mr. Miller."

"Call me Iron Man. Everyone does. Would you believe I'm sixty-three years old?"

Actually, I had no trouble believing it, thanks to the network of fine lines cross-hatching his spray tan—not to mention his thinning hair, dyed an unconvincing jet black.

"Incredible, isn't it?" he beamed with pride. "I've got the body of a twenty-year-old."

Better give it back, I felt like telling him. *You're getting it wrinkled.*

Then Chip uttered the magic words that set my heart flip-flopping.

"The salary is twenty thousand dollars."

"A fitness book! Really? How marvelous!"

Needless to say, I was no longer faking it.

"But before I can even consider hiring you," Chip said, reeling me down from Cloud Nine, "I need to give you a little quiz."

He then proceeded to bark out the following questions:

"Where are your deltoids?"

(No idea.)

"Your pecs?"

(No idea.)

"Your triceps?"

(Still no idea.)

I fumphered some answers, all of them wrong.

(Just FYI, your deltoids are nowhere near your big toe.)

Finally, he asked me, "What's your favorite machine at the gym?"

"The one that sells Snickers," I confessed.

What the heck? By this point, I was certain I was never going to get the gig.

But, much to my surprise, Chip beamed.

"Perfect! You're my target audience. If I can get somebody like you to write convincingly about the power of exercise, I can get *anyone* to try it!"

Hallelujah! I was the couch potato of his dreams.

"So when can you start?" he asked.

"Yesterday!" I cried, unable to tamp down my joy, thinking of those twenty thousand smackeroos winging their way to my checking account.

"I'm taking my family on an overnight trip to Santa Barbara tomorrow. Cancel whatever plans you've got. You're coming with us."

No worries there. No plans to cancel, unless you count my standing delivery order from Dominos.

"We're taking my private railway," Chip said.

Private railway? Yowser, this guy was loaded.

"There's nothing like seeing the country up close and personal, not looking down from a hunk of metal in the sky. We leave tomorrow afternoon at three from Union Station."

"I'll be there!"

But then I remembered a furry fly in my ointment: Prozac.

"I just have to find someone to look after my cat while I'm gone."

No easy task. My fractious furball has been banned from every kennel in town and claws my apartment to shreds if I leave her alone for a night.

"No worries. Bring your cat along."

"Really?"

"I insist!"

"I'm afraid she can be a bit of a handful."

Understatement of the century. That cat of mine gives Typhoid Mary a run for her money.

"No worries. I love cats. See you tomorrow."

And before I'd even gotten up from my seat, he was back on his Bluetooth, shouting orders at another hapless employee.

Somehow I managed to make my way through the maze of corridors to the front door. Outside, I practically skipped over to my Corolla, thrilled to have landed the gig, relieved that the only exercise I'd be getting would be banging away on my computer keyboard.

How wrong I was.

Little did I realize I'd soon be getting the workout of a lifetime, defending myself from a most inconvenient murder rap.

Chapter Two

Why, oh, why had I agreed to bring Prozac to Santa Barbara?

Trying to get Pro in her cat carrier is like trying to get me in a pair of Spanx—pure torture, a nightmare of screaming, screeching, and yowling.

And Prozac was making quite a racket, too.

The carrier was a deluxe model, the Ritz-Carlton of cat carriers, with a faux-mink lining and a special tray for kitty treats.

But the way Pro was carrying on, you'd think I was trying to give her a root canal without novocaine.

Yeowww! Unhand me this minute or I'm calling the ASPCA!

The fur was still flying when my neighbor Lance showed up. Fortunately, he'd offered to drive us to Union Station. (I could just picture an Uber driver tossing me and my wailing kitty to the curb at the first red light.)

"What's all the fuss?" Lance asked, strolling into my living room in jeans and a body-hugging tee, his blond curls moussed, as always, to perfection.

"This impossible cat is refusing to get in her carrier."

"Prozac, impossible? Not my little sweet pea. C'mon, hon."

With that, he picked her up and plopped her in the carrier, my duplicitous furball purring all the way.

Somehow she manages to turn on the charm for everyone but me.

"There," he said. "Easy-peasy. I don't understand why you're always complaining about Pro. She's a perfect angel."

A plaintive meow from the carrier.

You have no idea how I suffer under her tyrannical rule!

What a performance. Somebody get that cat an Oscar.

"Ready to go?" Lance asked.

"Just as soon as I wash the blood from my cat scratches."

Once my wounds had been disinfected, we made our way down the front path of the duplex Lance and I share on the outskirts of Beverly Hills.

Lance's bright red Mini Cooper was parked out front, and before long, we were whizzing along the freeway, Prozac curled up in her carrier in the back seat, docile as a geisha.

"Lucky you," Lance said, "heading off on a private railway to Santa Barbara, while I'm stuck here in town shoving bunions into Ferragamos."

The bunions to which he referred belong to the wealthy women who shop at Neiman Marcus, where Lance toils in the women's shoe department.

"So what's this job all about, anyway?"

"Chip Miller, owner of The Muscle Factory, has hired me to write a fitness book."

"You? Write a fitness book?" he cackled. "That's like asking Prozac to write a book about quantum physics."

An indignant meow from the back seat.

Hey, I could do it if I had opposable thumbs!

"For your information," I huffed, "Chip's very pumped about me. He's certain I've got what it takes to do the job."

Needless to say, I didn't tell him the part about how, as a confirmed couch potato, I was Chip's target audience.

"So, what's up with you?" I asked, eager to stave off a lecture about my nonexistent exercise routine.

"I've got good news and bad news. The good news is I've discovered a terrific way to meet boatloads of wealthy, sophisticated, urbane men."

"Move to San Francisco?"

"No, join the Empire Club."

"The Empire Club?"

"I've told you about it, haven't I?"

"Not that I recall."

Of course, it's very possible he told me, but I often tune Lance out when he's babbling about his search for Mr. Right—a search I've long abandoned after my disastrous marriage to my ex-husband (otherwise known as The Blob) and enough bad dates to qualify for a spot in the Guinness Book of Records.

"It's a private social club that just opened in West Hollywood," Lance was saying. "Lots of wealthy guys belong. They've got a dining room, spa, gym, and infinity pool—and they're always having parties and wine tastings. It's pricey, but definitely worth the investment."

"So what's the bad news?"

"I can't join unless I get someone to sponsor me. My boss at Neiman's is a member, and I've been hinting about how much I'd like to join, but so far, I've been getting nowhere, no matter how much I try to ingratiate myself with the guy."

Which is saying plenty. Lance practically has a PhD in bootlicking.

"That's too bad," I said

"No worries," Lance said. "I'll think of something."

Indeed he would. Something that would wind up driving me nuts, but I'll save that godawful adventure for another chapter.

Chapter Three

The minute Lance dropped us off at Union Station, Prozac reverted to prima-donna mode, yowling at the top of her lungs.

As I made my way across the cavernous Art Deco waiting room, Pro's screams echoing off the walls, people stopped to give me the stink eye—on the verge, no doubt, of reporting me to the pet police.

Even toddlers in the middle of their own tantrums paused to gaze at Prozac in admiration, clearly impressed by her lung power.

Finally, I arrived at the track where Chip's private railway cars had been attached to an Amtrak train. It was easy to spot Chip's three cars. While the rest of the train was an industrial gray, the last three cars were painted a deep magenta, with IRON MAN EXPRESS lettered in gold across each of them.

Thanks to this morning's cat carrier debacle, I was running a tad late and showed up at the train a few minutes after three.

A cute young steward was standing with a clipboard at the steps of the middle car.

"Welcome to the Iron Man Express!"

Tall and lanky, with the most appealing set of laugh

lines, he had the good looks of your typical boy next door, assuming the boy next door was a young William Holden.

"So sorry I'm late. I had some trouble getting my cat into her carrier this morning. She can be quite the drama queen."

Of course, now that a cute guy had appeared on the scene, Pro was back in geisha mode, all big green eyes and soft meows.

I have no idea what she's talking about.

"I'm Sean, and I'll be your steward for the trip," the cutie-pie said, checking his clipboard. "You must be Jaine Austen."

"Right."

"Love your books."

If I had a dollar for every time I heard that one, I'd be living in a villa in Saint-Tropez. Usually I try not to groan. But somehow when Sean said it, it seemed funny. Maybe it was the wink that came with it.

And I wasn't the only one impressed.

In her carrier, Pro was now purring her little heart out.

Hubba-hubba, hot stuff.

"And who might this be?"

She gazed up at him, batting her big green eyes.

Your future significant other if you play your cards right.

Flashing her a grin she didn't deserve, Sean took my bag and led us up the steps into the train.

"This is the sleeper car," he said, as we made our way along a carpeted hallway past mahogany-paneled cabins.

"The parlor car is up ahead, and the kitchen and dining room are right behind us."

"I didn't realize we'd be riding attached to an Amtrak train," I said.

"Yes, Amtrak allows private cars to be hooked up

to their trains. And once we get to Santa Barbara, Mr. Miller's cars will be shunted off to another track, one specially designated for cars not in transit."

It's amazing how convenient travel can be when you're filthy rich.

"Here's your room," Sean was saying, opening the door to a tiny but tastefully appointed cabin with a cozy window seat and twin-sized bed, the latter topped with a plush velvet coverlet and matching pillow sham.

A small door led to a private bathroom, complete with a litter box for Prozac.

By now, Pro was making a racket, demanding to be let out of her carrier. When I opened the latch, she hurled herself at Sean, writhing around his ankles in a mating frenzy.

"She certainly is a friendly little thing," Sean said, bending down to scratch her behind her ears.

Pro purred in ecstasy.

What do you think of inter-species relationships?

"I'd better be going," Sean said, prying Pro from his ankles. "Mr. Miller is waiting for you in the parlor car. He said to be sure to bring your cat."

Chip wasn't kidding when he told me he was a cat person. Which was a good thing, because I hated to think what havoc Pro might wreak on the velvet bedding if I left her alone.

"Remember," Sean said, "if you need anything, just ask."

A loud meow from Pro.

How about a big wet smacker?

And I must confess, looking at his eminently kissable laugh lines, I wouldn't have minded getting one myself.

Chapter Four

I stepped into the parlor car and blinked in awe at a domed ceiling gilded in what looked like real gold. Plush carpeting lay underfoot, and two rows of comfy swivel armchairs were lined up next to windows offering a panoramic view of the California coast.

At one end of the car was a bar; at the other, a potted palm and an intricately woven tapestry.

Several of the swivel chairs, I noticed, were accessorized with throw pillows that said WORLD'S BEST DAD.

Chip was sitting at the far end of the car in a chair closest to the tapestry, a laptop on a work table in front of him, his feet pumping away at an under-the-desk bike.

Seated next to him was a paunchy bald guy in his forties and a brassy blonde with an imposing set of what had to be surgically enhanced boobs.

Across the aisle, a gal with long Botticelli curls sat cross-legged in her chair, eyes closed, a crystal resting in her upturned palms.

Just as he'd been on the day I met him, Chip was once again barking orders—this time to the rosy-cheeked maid who'd greeted me at his spread in Bel Air. Today, I was somewhat surprised to see that, instead of an apron, she sported a pink sweatshirt with the words I BELIEVE IN

CHOCOLATE FOR BREAKFAST embroidered across her ample chest.

"Tell the chef I want the steaks rare. Blood rare."

"But, Dad," said the paunchy guy, "I like my steak medium rare."

"Me, too," said the blonde.

Me, too, I felt like chiming in.

"Too bad," Chip snapped. "My train, my rules."

Then he spotted me standing at the other end of the car.

"C'mere, Jaine!" he cried, waving me over. "How do you like this parlor car? It once belonged to Cornelius Vanderbilt II. Paid three hundred grand to have it refurbished."

"It's amazing," I said, heading over to join the others, still bowled over by that gold ceiling.

"Everybody, meet Jaine Austen, the writer I hired to help me with my book."

"Hell, no!" cried the paunchy guy, looking at Pro in alarm. "She brought a cat?"

"Her name's Prozac," I offered with a weak smile.

"For crying out loud, Dad. You know I'm allergic to cats."

And indeed, his eyes were already beginning to water.

"Ridiculous," Chip replied with a dismissive wave. "Your allergies are all in your mind."

But I got the distinct impression he was enjoying his son's discomfort.

"Jaine, this fella faking allergies is my son Cory."

Cory gave me a desultory nod.

"His wife, Bree," Chip continued.

The brassy blonde managed a tepid approximation of a smile.

"And my daughter Cassidy."

The chick with the Botticelli curls seemed lost in a trance, staring out into space.

"She's meditating," Cory said, with a major eye roll.

"And finally," Chip said, indicating the older rosy-cheeked woman, "this is my sister, Versel Diane Rush."

His sister? The way he'd talked to her, I assumed she was his maid.

"VD for short," Chip added with a chuckle.

"My brother gets his jollies referring to me as a venereal disease," said Versel, offering me the first genuine smile I'd gotten so far.

"Okay," Chip snapped at the others. "Everybody scram. I want to get started on my book."

Versel roused Cassidy from her meditative trance, and they all filed out, Cory eyeing one of the WORLD'S BEST DAD throw pillows in disgust.

"Let's see that cat of yours," Chip said, once the others were gone.

Gingerly, I put Pro in his arms.

She gazed up at him through slitted eyes, unimpressed.

He's not nearly as cute as Sean.

It looked like she was about to wriggle free, but then Chip started scratching her behind her ears, and she melted into a puddle in his lap.

She's always been a slut for an ear scratch.

"Did you bring anything to take notes?" Chip asked.

"Sure did," I replied, taking a steno pad from my purse, along with my cell phone.

"I'll be recording our sessions, too."

"Great! I've already thought of a terrific title. *From Flab to Fab in Ten Easy Lessons!*"

A definite D minus for fat shaming, but I had to admit it sounded sort of snappy.

Maybe working with Chip would be a fun experience.

No such luck, as I was about to discover.

"I thought I'd start out with an introduction," Chip said, "about my philosophy of exercise and my meteoric rise to success."

And he was off and running on an egomaniacal rant, blathering about his early years, working three jobs to put himself through community college. About single-handedly building his business from the ground up, from a tiny storefront in Hollywood to a chain of gyms across the country. About his business acuity and his philanthropy. Even about his prowess as a lover.

To hear him tell it, he was a combination of Hercules, Casanova, and Bill Gates.

It was a good thing I was recording it all, because before long my mind started wandering, thinking about that steak we'd be getting for dinner. I could always eat around the bloody part. And surely, there'd be some kind of potato on the plate. Maybe baked. Or scalloped. Not to mention dinner rolls, wine, and dessert.

While I was conducting an internal debate about what I'd rather have for my dream dessert (banana cream pie or chocolate mousse cake), I saw Prozac jump down off Chip's lap and scamper behind his swivel chair.

Chip was so engrossed in his ode to himself, he didn't even notice.

The minutes continued to slog by as Chip droned on and on.

I'd long since resolved the dessert debate (as always, chocolate won) and Chip was still gassing away. Finally, just when I thought I'd sprain my neck from nodding at his chatter, I heard the blessed words:

"That's it for today. I'm off for a power nap. See you and Prozac at cocktail hour."

And off he strode to the sleeper car.

I checked my watch. Had only forty-five minutes passed? It seemed like centuries.

I was tempted to tiptoe to the bar to get a head start on cocktail hour, but afraid of making a bad impression if caught in the act, I decided to return to my cabin.

I looked around for Prozac, but she was nowhere in sight. For a frightening instant, I panicked. Had she somehow managed to dash out of the parlor car, only to wind up stuck between cars, clinging for dear life by her claws?

I was flooded with relief when at last I spotted her behind Chip's chair.

But my relief quickly turned to dismay when I saw she was clawing away at the ornate wall tapestry.

I bent down to take a closer look and saw loose threads dangling.

Pro gazed up at me, with an enthusiastic thump of her tail.

What a nifty scratching post. I want one for our apartment.

"Prozac!" I groaned. "Look what you've done!"

Impressive, isn't it?

Thank heavens I'd packed a pair of miniature travel scissors. I'd come back later that night after everyone had gone to sleep and snip off the offending threads. I just hoped no one would notice they were missing. In the meanwhile, I pushed the faux potted palm in front of Prozac's handiwork and sprinted back to my cabin, cursing Pro all the way.

You've Got Mail!

To: Jausten
From: Shoptillyoudrop
Subject: So much news!

So much news to report, honey. Yesterday Tampa Vistas res-
ident Mildred Kimble turned one hundred, and we had a
lovely luncheon for her at the clubhouse. Mildred was so
cute. When asked how she felt about turning one hundred,
she said, "Oh, to be ninety-nine again!"

What's more, the Tampa Vistas annual costume party is just
around the corner. Everyone is so excited! I'm going in the
same 1920's flapper dress I wore last year. (Only $69.99 plus
shipping and handling from the Home Shopping Channel!) I
got so many compliments, I can't resist wearing it again.

I've absolutely forbidden Daddy to wear the costume he
wore last year. He came as a pirate with a fake parrot
strapped to his shoulder. But the strap broke and the parrot
fell smack into Edna Lindstrom's Swedish meatballs.
Needless to say no one went near the meatballs except
Daddy, who, after plucking a few parrot feathers out of the
dish, practically polished off the whole platter. Poor Edna
was inconsolable.

But I'm getting sidetracked from the most exciting news of
all. Just got a phone call from darling Lydia Pinkus, president
of the Homeowners Association, who had her DNA tested,
and guess what? It turns out she's a direct descendant of
Betsy Ross! Imagine that!

She's coming to the party dressed as Betsy and is sure to win the Best Costume prize, as she does every year.

Must run. Have to tell Daddy the good news about Lydia!

XOXO,
Mom

To: Jausten
From: DaddyO
Subject: Revolting news!

Revolting news, Lambchop. Apparently Lydia Pinkus, aka The Battle-Axe and despotic president of the homeowners association, had her DNA tested and is a direct descendant of Betsy Ross. My God, the woman's always been a blowhard, with her rules and regulations and mind-numbing educational lectures. Now that she found out she's a descendant of someone famous, she's going to be more insufferable than ever.

No way am I showing up at the costume party to watch her swan around as a glorified seamstress. I'm boycotting the party and staying home to watch Sylvester Stallone play a true American hero—Rambo! And nothing, absolutely nothing, will get me to change my mind.

Love 'n snuggles from
Daddy

To: Jausten
From: Shoptillyoudrop
Subject: No More Meatloaf!

Now Daddy's refusing to come to the costume party. I told him if he refused to go, I'd never make him meatloaf again.

XOXO,
Mom

To: Jausten
From: DaddyO
Subject: Slight Change of Plans

Slight change of plans, Lambchop. In a power play she no doubt learned from The Battle-Axe, Mom's refusing to cook me meatloaf ever again unless I come to the costume party.

And you know how much I love your mom's meatloaf.

So I'm going to the party. But it will be a hollow victory for Mom. I refuse to put an ounce of effort into my costume. I've decided to wear my robe and pajamas and come as Hugh Hefner.

Love 'n hugs
from your put-upon
Daddy

P.S. Two can play at this ancestry game. I've just sent my DNA off to be tested. I wouldn't be at all surprised if I was descended from Henry VIII. After all, even though everyone calls me Hank, my real name is Henry, and I did have six girl-friends before I married your mom. True, three of those girl-friends were in my kindergarten class, but they still count.

Chapter Five

"What on earth am I going to do with you?" I scolded Prozac once we were back in the cabin.

How about a nice relaxing belly rub? That works for me.

"Forget it," I said, tossing her onto the cabin's window seat.

Then I carefully stowed the bed's velvet coverlet and pillow sham in a storage drawer under the bed.

Prozac glared at me, miffed.

Hey, I was counting on shredding that stuff to smithereens.

"You've done enough damage for one day, young lady."

Once the cabin was Prozac-proofed, I checked my cell phone and was happy to see I had a Wi-Fi connection. But then I made the foolhardy mistake of reading my parents' emails, an exercise usually guaranteed to send my blood pressure spiking.

Ever since my parents retired to Florida so Mom could be closer to her beloved Home Shopping Channel, Daddy has had it in for Lydia Pinkus, aka The Battle-Axe, and president of the Tampa Vistas Homeowners Association.

I've met Lydia a few times, and I have to admit she has the unnerving air of a well-bred Rottweiler.

Daddy has always chafed under Lydia's iron rule, engaging in a never-ending game of "Anything You Can Do, I Can Do Better."

(And the answer to that refrain is always, "No, he can't.")

I only hoped this ancestry thing wouldn't blow up into World War III.

But I couldn't squander any more mental energy on my parents; I had troubles enough of my own. Namely that bald spot on Chip's tapestry.

Shoving all negative thoughts from my mind, I curled up on the bed, hoping to take a de-stressing nap.

Prozac, as she always does when she senses I'm upset, stayed as far away from me as possible on the window seat, treating me to a scenic view of her tush.

I swear, I'd get more empathy from a guppy.

I tried lulling myself to sleep with a meditation app, but the silken-voiced meditation lady instructed me to picture myself lying on a beach under swaying palm trees, listening to the soothing slap of the waves against the shore, and feeling the warm sun caressing my body.

But every time I tried to picture myself lying on a beach, I kept getting bogged down in thoughts of what I was supposed to wear. A bathing suit was out of the question; no way was I about to expose my thighs in public, no matter how soft the breezes or how warm the sun. I could wear capris and a tee, or maybe a sundress, or Bermuda shorts, if they weren't too short. I was getting so stressed about what to wear to my imaginary beach, I clicked off the app and tried to meditate on my own, picturing hot fudge sauce being drizzled over a bowl of Chunky Monkey ice cream.

But even that delightful image couldn't erase the thought of that damn tapestry.

Maybe I should come clean and tell Chip what happened. After all, it was just a few loose threads. Surely he'd understand.

Or not. From what I'd seen so far, he didn't exactly seem like an understanding kind of guy. And I couldn't afford to jeopardize my twenty-thousand-dollar paycheck. Besides, Chip was the one who insisted I bring Prozac on board in the first place. So, I thought, doing some frantic rationalizing, the whole tapestry fiasco was Chip's fault anyway.

By now, I'd totally given up on that nap idea. It was time to seek solace from my good buddy, Mr. Chardonnay. So I grabbed Pro and started off for the parlor car to get a head start on happy hour.

I perked up considerably when I saw Sean at the bar, setting out some munchies. And I wasn't the only one who liked what she saw.

In my arms, Prozac was purring on overdrive.

Well, hello, big boy.

Then she noticed a bowl of caviar Sean had just set down on the bar. She looked back and forth from Sean to the caviar, no doubt trying to decide which was yummier.

In the end, she opted for the chow.

(She takes after me that way.)

Now she was wriggling in my arms, desperate to break free and swan dive into the caviar.

"Prozac!" I chided. "Behave yourself."

"She wants that caviar," I explained to Sean.

"Is that so?" he said, scratching her behind her ears. "Your wish is my command, Princess Prozac."

With that, he took a caviar spoon and fed her a healthy dollop. She scarfed it down at the speed of light and started meowing for more.

"That's enough, princess," Sean said. "*No mas.*"

Normally, she'd wail at the top of her lungs until she got what she wanted, but not then.

Instead, she looked up at Sean all gooey-eyed and obedient.

If you say so, sugar lips.

"Want some caviar?" he asked me.

"No, thanks. I've never really liked the stuff."

"Me, neither," he said, smoothing over the crater in the caviar left by Prozac's snack. "Give me a frank in a blanket any day."

"You like franks in a blanket?"

"My favorite appetizer."

"Mine, too!" I practically squealed in delight. "It's so rare to find people these days who appreciate a classic frank in a blanket."

"Tell me about it. I don't get the whole sushi thing, either. I mean, who wants to eat raw fish?"

Okay, it was official. Prozac wasn't the only one falling in love with the guy.

"Can I get you something to drink?" he asked.

"I'd love some chardonnay."

"There doesn't seem to be any here," he said, rummaging behind the bar. "I know we've got plenty in the wine cooler in the kitchen. I'll go get you some."

He was about to head for the door when Versel showed up, a tote bag on her arm.

"Hello, Mrs. Rush," he said, greeting her with a warm smile.

"Please. Mrs. Rush is my late nightmare of a mother-in-law. Call me Versel."

"I was just going to the kitchen to get Jaine some chardonnay. Can I get you some, too? There doesn't seem to be any here at the bar."

"That's because my brother makes everyone drink his Iron Man Martini at happy hour."

"You think he'd mind if I brought Jaine a glass of wine?"

"Probably. With Chip, it's his way or the highway."

"Better forget it," I said, thinking of those loose threads in the tapestry and how I couldn't afford to get on Chip's bad side.

"Okay, then," Sean said. "See you at dinner, ladies."

Pro and I stared after him wistfully as he left.

"Such a nice young man," Versel said.

Prozac shot her a withering glare.

Hands off, sister. He's mine!

Oblivious to Prozac's ire, Versel settled down on one of the swivel chairs and took out some knitting from her tote bag.

I sat down next to her, and immediately Prozac began trying to wriggle her way off my lap.

"She wants that caviar," I explained to Versel.

"Bad idea. Nobody's allowed to touch the caviar until Chip shows up. He likes to take the inaugural spoonful."

Yikes. What a control freak. I prayed he wouldn't smell the caviar on Pro's breath.

"Settle down, Prozac," Versel said firmly, watching Pro squirm in my lap.

And just like that, Pro stopped wriggling.

Why does that cat listen to everyone on the planet but me?

It had been hours since I'd scarfed down lunch, and by now I was feeling more than a tad peckish.

"Care for a pretzel?" Versel asked, as if reading my mind.

She reached into her tote and pulled out a bag of the salty treats.

"I smuggle them aboard all the time. Chip doesn't approve of empty calories."

"Thank you!" I cried, taking one and chomping down on it with gusto.

"Have some more," she offered, my rescuing angel.

"Maybe just one," I replied, grabbing a handful.

"So how did your session with Chip go this afternoon?"

"Very interesting," I lied.

"Oh, please. I bet he chewed your ear off, bragging about himself. Did he tell you how he single-handedly turned a tiny storefront gym into an exercise empire?"

"Yes, he did."

In excruciating detail were the words I tactfully refrained from adding.

"Total BS. Chip's first partner, Scotty Dickens, was the brains behind the company, the one who turned it into a nationwide chain, only to walk away with two weeks' severance pay after Chip and his henchmen lawyers screwed him over."

Ouch. The more I learned about Chip, the less I liked him. In fact, by now I sort of loathed the guy.

"He's my brother," Versel was saying, "and he's been good to me, taking me in after my husband died, but he can be a mean SOB. Not to mention a raging egomaniac."

She pointed to a throw pillow on one of the swivel chairs.

"See all these WORLD'S BEST DAD pillows? Chip bought them himself. Yep, my brother's a piece of work, all right. All I can say is, don't get on his bad side."

Now more than ever, I prayed he wouldn't discover Prozac's handiwork on his tapestry.

"So who else is on board the train?" I asked, eager to steer clear of any more Chip chatter.

"You've already met Cory and Bree, Chip's son and daughter-in-law. And my niece, Cassidy."

I nodded, remembering their tepid welcome.

"There's Chip's girlfriend, Avery. Avery Suzuki Tomkins Feinberg, to be precise. We call her The Widowmaker because all three of her husbands died, and the last two left her a small fortune. She's a bit of an ice queen. Except with Chip, of course. Then she turns up the flame to hot, hot, hot.

"And Denny Sullivan's on board, too. He's Chip's right-hand man at the gym. Got his nose so far up Chip's fanny, I wouldn't be surprised if he found a few polyps.

"As for the staff, there's Sean, our steward, and the chef, Mario. I don't really know much about either of them. Cassidy hired them both through a domestic agency."

Gradually, the others started wandering in. First, Bree and Cory—who took one look at Prozac and groaned.

"Dammit. Not that cat again."

"I'm so sorry," I said. "Your dad didn't tell me you were allergic to cats."

"Of course he didn't," Cory said, sitting as far from me as possible. "The man lives to make me miserable."

"Here, hon," Versel said, reaching into her copious tote. "I've got some Benadryl."

"Thanks, Aunt Versel, but I already took some."

"Anybody want a pretzel?" Versel offered.

Both Bree and Cory shook their heads *no*.

"Maybe just a couple," I said, embarrassed that I was the only taker. But that didn't stop me from grabbing some.

Cassidy drifted in next, her Botticelli curls cascading down the back of a gauzy maxi dress.

"Hi, there!" she said, catching sight of me. "Who're you?"

"You've already met," Versel pointed out. "You were in a meditative trance at the time."

"I'm Jaine Austen. I'm helping your dad write his book."

"You're a writer? Neat! I'm an artist myself. I do oils mostly, some watercolors. I always love connecting with other creative people," she said, gracing me with a warm smile. "Welcome aboard!"

At least she was pleasant. I liked her.

"You really shouldn't be eating those," she added, eyeing the pretzel I was about to shove in my mouth. "Carbs and salt. Total poison."

Sanctimonious killjoy. Maybe I didn't like her so much, after all.

"Good evening, everyone."

I turned to see an elegant Asian woman coming into the parlor car. Perfectly put together in a silky black lounge set, her delicate features framed by a flawless, chin-length bob, she was a *Vogue* cover come to life.

She could have been anywhere between thirty and sixty, depending on how many visits she'd paid to her plastic surgeon.

I figured she was Chip's girlfriend, The Widowmaker.

Cory and Bree merely grunted, while Cassidy managed a lackluster "Hey, Avery."

"Avery, I'd like you to meet Jaine Austen," Versel said. "She's working with Chip on his book."

The Widowmaker offered me a cool and somewhat bony hand. "How lovely to meet you. And how lucky you are to be working with Chip."

"Oh, please," Cory snickered. "Chances are she'll quit before the trip is over. My dad goes through writers like he goes through chefs."

"And girlfriends," Bree added with a vicious gleam in her eye.

Avery lobbed her a sly mile.

"Bea, how lovely to see you and *your* girlfriends," she said, staring at Bree's silicone boobs. "I'm surprised they don't need a cabin of their own."

Bree bristled.

"It's Bree, not Bea!"

"Ignore her," Cory said to his wife. "She's just trying to get a rise out of you."

"My God, it's so toxic in here," Cassidy said, cross-legged on her swivel chair. "Can't everybody just chillax? If you all meditated fifteen a minutes a day, you'd have a much more positive mindset."

"Give us a break," Cory snapped. "You and your endless preaching about meditation are about as irritating as that damn cat."

In my lap, Prozac meowed, indignant.

How dare you? I'm much more irritating than her!

Eager to break up what looked like an impending cage match, Versel asked Avery, "So where's Chip?"

"Probably still in his cabin, taking his power nap."

How interesting, I thought. Seemed like Chip and Avery slept in separate cabins.

"Chip insists on taking a power nap every day," Versel explained to me. "Claims it keeps him young."

And indeed, as he entered the parlor just then, he did seem quite bright-eyed and bushy-tailed.

"Hello, doll," he said, giving Avery a sloppy kiss on the mouth—a PDA I certainly could have done without.

"Okay," he said when he'd pried his lips from Avery's, "time for Iron Man Martinis!"

With that, he darted behind the bar and took out a ginormous shaker, into which he poured ice cubes, a copious amount of gin, and the merest trace of vermouth.

As he began to shake the concoction, a buff, forty-something guy with a buzz cut and muscles galore came bounding in to join us.

"Sorry I'm late, Chip. Just finished ordering the new treadmills."

I figured he must be Denny, Chip's second-in-command.

"Denny, my man!" Chip said. "C'mere and help me put olives in these martinis."

Denny joined Chip behind the bar, spearing olives with toothpicks and dropping them into the martinis.

"Ta-da!" Chip said when the martinis were lined up on the bar. "The Iron Man Martini!"

He was beaming with such pride, you'd think he'd just invented the crockpot.

"They look divine," Avery said, with a silky smile.

At least he had one fan in the group.

"Chop chop, VD," Chip snapped. "Help us hand out the drinks."

With a sigh, Versel got up from her chair to do her brother's bidding.

Soon everyone was clutching one of Chip's extra-strength gin bombs.

Chip held up his glass in a toast.

"Here's to those who wish me well," he boomed. "All the rest can go to hell!"

Oh, boy. Looked like it was going to be Standing Room Only in purgatory.

Chapter Six

Somehow I managed to glug down a few sips of what had to be the world's strongest martini. I suspected the stuff could double as paint thinner.

And it didn't help that the olive, as I was to discover once I'd popped it in my mouth, was stuffed with jalapeño pepper.

My throat was on fire as Chip proceeded to dominate the conversation, singing his own praises.

When everyone was sufficiently anesthetized, from the gin and Chip's ode to himself, we trooped over to the dining car, where a spacious table was set with white linen and gleaming silver.

Chip sat at the head of the table, with Avery on his right and Denny at his left.

I was grateful to be seated out of Chip's orbit, between Versel and Cassidy at the other end of the table, Cory and Bree sitting across from us—a food bowl for Prozac on the floor at my feet.

A swinging door with a small window led to the attached kitchen. I figured the window was there to let Sean know when it was time to bring out the chow.

I was busy gulping down my water, trying to put out the

jalapeño fire in my throat, when Sean began pouring everyone champagne.

Once we each had a glass in front of us, Chip clinked his with a spoon.

"Great news, everybody!" he boomed. "I've asked Avery to marry me, and she's said yes!"

Next to him, Avery beamed.

"And here's a little something to seal the deal."

With that, he handed Avery a velvet jewelry box.

"Oh, Chip!" she cried, taking out an ice cube-sized diamond and slipping it on her slender finger. "It's gorgeous. You've made me the happiest woman in the world."

"Dream on, honey," Versel muttered under her breath. "Three months living with Chip and you'll have your divorce attorney on speed dial."

Chip's "great news" was not exactly greeted with glee. Cory sat there, jaw clenched, while Bree eyed Avery's rock with unabashed envy. Cassidy seemed unfazed by the news, a Buddha-like smile on her face, probably lost in one of her meditative trances. Either that, or she was zonked out from her Iron Man Martini.

Only Denny was bursting with enthusiasm.

"To the happy couple!" he said, raising his glass. "To Avery, whose beauty outshines the gem on her finger. And to Chip, as I described him in my recent interview with *Gymnastics Today*, 'the best boss a guy could ever work for!'"

Was it my imagination, or did I see a flicker of annoyance cross Chip's face as Denny gave his toast?

I was more than a tad peckish at this point, with only those pretzels and jalapeño-stuffed olive rattling around in my tummy. So you can imagine my disappointment when the first course turned out to be an anemic green salad.

(Hey, if I wanted green food, I'd be eating pistachio ice cream.)

Here and there were a few chunks of feta cheese, which I plucked out and inhaled at the speed of light.

At my feet, Prozac was scarfing down de-luscious steak tidbits. It took every ounce of willpower I possessed not to reach down and grab one.

By now we'd arrived in Santa Barbara, where the Iron Man Express had been shunted off to an area reserved for private railway cars. Outside the moon was bright in the sky, and in the distance I could see it casting shimmering pinpricks of light on the ocean.

But the view I was most interested in was that of Sean, when he finally showed up to serve our main course: juicy steaks, with mashed potatoes and asparagus spears.

True, my steak was a tad too rare for me, but I ate it anyway and dug into those mashed potatoes with gusto.

Next to me, Cassidy ignored her steak and potatoes, mumbling something about how they were "a heart attack on a plate." Instead she pecked at her asparagus spears, claiming she was "stuffed" from her salad.

The woman was really beginning to get on my nerves.

Meanwhile, Prozac had finished inhaling her steak and was now yowling for more.

I was hoping Chip would banish her to our cabin, but no such luck. Instead, he summoned her onto his lap, where she spent the rest of the meal alternately snoozing and scarfing down steak tidbits from Chip.

I never did get that glass of chardonnay I'd been lusting after; Chip decreed only red wine would be served at dinner. But I must confess it was quite yummy. A major improvement over that turpentine martini.

Sean was going around the table, topping off everyone's glass, when he accidentally spilled the tiniest drop of wine at Versel's place setting.

"I'm so sorry!" Sean said.

"Not a problem," Versel assured him.

"Of course, it's a problem!" Chip snapped. "He just spilled red wine on my white tablecloth. If I can't get it out, you're paying for a replacement, kid."

Yikes. If Chip was this angry over a mere jot of wine, I shuddered to think how he'd react to Prozac's handiwork on his tapestry. Fortunately the damage was at the bottom, close to the floor. I was still hoping that if I cut off the loose threads, he'd never even notice.

I was lost in thoughts of my upcoming tapestry surgery when Chip once more clinked his glass, calling for our attention, announcing tomorrow's activity schedule.

"We're going kayak racing in the morning, followed by lunch at my favorite winery, then back home to L.A."

Wait, what? Did Chip just say *kayak racing*?

"So don't forget to bring your bathing suits!"

Absolutely not. You know how I feel about wearing a bathing suit in public, with my thighs on display for all the world to see.

"I'm so sorry, Chip," I piped up, "but I won't be able to go kayaking. I didn't bring a bathing suit."

"I'll buy you one at the kayak shop."

"But what about Prozac? Shouldn't I stay here on the train to take care of her?"

"Not a problem. Sean will watch her."

An enthusiastic meow from Pro, who gazed up adoringly at Sean.

Yes! Come to Mama, big boy!

First the tapestry fiasco, now this bathing suit thing.

I was so miserable, I couldn't even finish the flourless chocolate cake Sean served for dessert.

(Okay, so I finished it. And part of Cassidy's, too, if you must know.)

When I'd scraped the last crumb of chocolate from my plate, Chip summoned the chef from the kitchen.

He was a handsome guy with slicked back hair and a growth of bad boy stubble on his chiseled face. The kind of chill hipster you see in tequila commercials.

But as handsome as he was, I was still a fervent member of Team Sean, whose boyish good looks were the kind that made my heart do somersaults.

"My compliments to the chef," Chip said.

"Thank you, sir." The chef smiled modestly.

"Not you, Mario," Chip amended with a sly smirk. "But to the chef who somewhere tonight served a decent meal. Your meal, I'm afraid, left quite a bit to be desired. The steaks should've been bloodier, the mashed potatoes needed more butter, the asparagus spears weren't al dente enough, and the chocolate cake could've been more chocolate-y."

Ouch. Talk about your low blows.

Mario nodded stiffly and marched back to the kitchen.

Why did I get the feeling that Chip's next meal would be laced with a gourmet dollop of spit?

Chapter Seven

After dinner, Chip proposed we adjourn to the parlor car to play Trivial Pursuit.

"I bet I win," he boasted. "I always do!"

"That's because he's memorized all the answers on the cards," Versel whispered to me.

Wow. The man had the moral compass of a Nigerian Internet prince.

"Sorry, Chip," Versel said. "I'm bushed. I'm turning in for the night."

"Me, too," echoed Cory, Bree, and Cassidy.

And off they scurried to their cabins.

The last thing I wanted to do was play Trivial Pursuit with Chip, but I needed to stay in the parlor car until the place had cleared out and get started on Operation Tapestry Repair.

So, after dropping off Prozac in my cabin, I trotted over to the parlor car to match wits with Chip, Avery, and Denny.

I suppose mine has been a spotty education. The only answers I knew in Trivial Pursuit were "Arts & Literature" and "Movies & Entertainment." I was pretty hopeless when it came to Sports, Geography, and History. Denny,

I noted, was even worse than me, scoring only when the topic was sports.

Avery, however, was a smart cookie with an education far more well-rounded than mine. She would've beat Chip for sure if he hadn't memorized all the answers.

And BTW, every time he got an answer right, which was *all* the time, he shouted, "Iron Man Scores!"

Fifteen minutes into the game, I was ready to throttle him.

We played for about an hour, which flew by like a decade.

At last, Chip won and declared with a lascivious wink that it was time for him and Avery to retire to his cabin to celebrate their engagement.

For some reason I'll never understand, Avery did not seem revolted at the prospect of tumbling into bed with Iron Man. In my humble op, the woman deserved combat pay for even kissing the guy.

We all bid each other good night, Denny sucking up to Chip mercilessly, yakking about his bravura performance at Trivial Pursuit.

I returned to my cabin to find Prozac napping, not a care in the world.

"This is all your fault," I chided her, rooting around in my overnight case for my trusty travel scissors.

But she was too busy snoring to hear a word I said.

Once I found the scissors, I tiptoed back to the parlor car.

It was pitch dark when I showed up. Unwilling to risk drawing attention by turning on the lights, I used my cell phone to light my way to the tapestry at the far end of the car, where I was heartened to see only a few loose threads.

I was just reaching for my scissors to snip them to oblivion when I heard the parlor car door open.

I quickly shut off my flashlight and crouched down behind a swivel chair.

Whoever had arrived turned on the light over the bar, leaving the rest of the parlor car dark. Luckily I was hidden in the shadows.

"God, I need a drink."

"Me, too."

I recognized the voices right away. It was Cory and Bree.

"Scotch, rocks?" Cory asked.

"Make it a double."

I heard the clink of ice cubes, then the glug of scotch being poured into glasses.

Peeking from behind the swivel chair, I saw them both sink down into seats near the bar.

"I can't believe he asked Avery to marry him," Cory moaned. "What if there's no prenup? What if he changes his will and leaves her everything?"

I was expecting Bree to comfort him, but that wasn't about to happen.

"Actually," she said, her voice as chilly as the ice in her scotch, "I don't intend to stick around to find out."

"What are you talking about?" Cory asked, alarmed.

"Before we got married, you promised me you were going to be named CEO of The Muscle Factory. But it's been two years, and you're still little more than a glorified errand boy. If you can't oust your dad and get control of the company in the next thirty days, I'm filing for divorce."

"Bree, you can't mean that."

"Look, Cory, you know I love you."

That I found highly doubtful.

"But I can't live under your dad's thumb any more. Face it, sweetheart. I'm hot, and I'm sure I can do better than this. Get control of the company or I'm gone."

She slugged down her drink, slammed the empty glass on the bar, then started for the door.

"I'll do it!" Cory cried, hurrying after her. "I swear, I'll get rid of him."

Words I'd remember loud and clear in the days to come.

The minute they were gone, I crept back to the tapestry, turned on my flashlight, and snipped off the offending threads. There was a tiny bald spot, but it was hardly noticeable, and I was keeping my fingers crossed that Chip wouldn't discover it. I was about to get up and head back to my cabin when I heard the parlor car door opening again.

Holy mackerel. It was like Grand Central Station in here.

I turned off my flashlight and ducked back down behind the swivel chair.

Peeking out from behind my hiding spot, I saw Chip in a plush terry robe, and Denny in sweats.

"I gotta thank you, Chip, for inviting me on this trip," Denny was saying. "What a great way to travel! But what are we doing here in the parlor car? I thought you were 'celebrating' with Avery."

"I was," Chip crowed. "We did. Iron Man scored!"

Poor Avery. Not much foreplay in that celebration.

"Way to go!" Denny said, ever the toady.

"Do you have any idea why I asked you here?" Chip said.

"To give me that raise you've been promising me?"

"Guess again, hot shot. You're fired."

"Fired?" Denny gulped, his eyes wide with disbelief. "You gotta be kidding! After all I've done for you? Who got you those factory-second treadmills from Bangladesh at a fraction of what you would've paid here in the States? And what about all the great stuff I said about you in my interview with *Gymnastics Today*!"

Chip stiffened at the mention of the magazine.

"And just who gave you permission to do that interview?" he snapped. "I sure didn't."

"I didn't think I'd need your permission to do a puff piece on you."

"You thought wrong. The only one who talks to the press about Iron Man is Iron Man. Nobody who tries to steal my thunder gets to stay on my payroll. Consider yourself terminated."

"You son of a bitch! I've been sweating bullets, working sixteen-hour days, and this is how you repay me?"

Apparently so.

"You've got two weeks to clear out. No severance pay."

In the overhead light of the bar area, I could see Denny's face flushed with anger.

"You're not going to get away with this," he said through gritted teeth.

"Don't even try to sue. My lawyers will crush you. You'll be drowning in legal fees before you know what hit you. Just pack your things and leave in the morning."

"No way, Chip. I'm staying on this train till the bitter end. I intend to eat your food and drink your wine and beat the hell out of you at kayaking tomorrow. You wanna get me off this train, you're gonna have to call the police. And I don't think you want that kind of publicity."

"Okay, stick around," Chip shrugged. "It's your funeral."

"Au contraire, buddy. It's your funeral. I'm gonna see to that."

Once again, words I would not soon forget.

Chapter Eight

I checked out my reflection in the dressing room of the Kayak Adventures gift shop and groaned in dismay.

My body had been crammed into a Size None of Your Business Speedo. On the plus side, the swimsuit's industrial-strength spandex smoothed out my tummy. On the minus side, it shoved all my excess tummy goop to my tush and thighs.

How lucky Pro was, I thought, back on the train with Sean. I'd left her ecstatic in his arms, purring up a storm.

"Thanks so much for watching her," I'd said to Sean.

"No worries," he assured me. "Just have fun today."

Pro wriggled with delight.

I intend to, hot stuff!

Now I was here at the Santa Barbara harbor, stuck in spandex hell.

I'd begged Chip to let me buy shorts and a tee, but he insisted on a bathing suit.

The guy clearly was getting his jollies watching me squirm.

And that made me mad.

I decided then and there not to let him win this little mind game.

So I stiffened my spine and, with head held high, walked

out of the dressing room and onto the beach, owning my body and unashamed of my extra pounds.

And guess what? The world did not stop on its axis. On the contrary. Versel, seated in a beach chair next to Avery, looked me over and nodded in approval.

"Hey, sexy lady!" she winked.

She and Avery had been granted special dispensation to stay behind and watch the kayak race.

"I can't go because I have a bad case of MMB," Versel said.

"MMB?"

"Make Believe Bursitis. I use it to get out of all Chip-related sports activities."

Darn it. Why hadn't I thought of something clever like that?

"What about you, Avery?" I asked. "How come you're not kayaking?"

Looking elegant in a miraculously unwrinkled linen blouse and pants, her engagement ring blinding in the morning sun, Avery explained that Chip wanted her to stay behind so that she could watch him in action.

Better watching him in action here at the beach than in his bed.

Meanwhile, the others were milling around, donning life jackets. Aside from me and Cory—with his burgeoning pot belly—all them were in terrific shape.

Bree was a Barbie doll come to life, with her surgically enhanced boobs, tiny waist, and slender legs. Which just goes to show what good genes, careful diet, and five hours a day at the gym can do for a gal.

Even ethereal Cassidy, whom I expected to be willowy and frail, was totally ripped, her body sculpted to perfection.

Of course, Chip and Denny were walking advertisements for The Muscle Factory—Denny a decades younger, wrinkle-free edition of his about-to-be ex-boss.

But Chip's slack skin didn't stop him from strutting around like the Incredible Hulk with liver spots.

"Do I have to wear this silly life jacket?" Bree was whining. "It's so bulky."

"That bimbo doesn't need a life jacket," Versel muttered. "With that chest, she'll never drown."

Bidding adieu to Versel and Avery, I joined the others to get a life jacket. A helpful Kayak Adventures employee named Jason, learning that I'd never gone kayaking before, showed me how to use a paddle, rotating it from side to side.

Standing there on the shore, paddling in the air, it seemed easy.

Who knew? I might turn out to be good at this kayaking stuff. After all, my arms were pretty darn strong from hauling pints of Chunky Monkey home from the supermarket.

"Listen up, everybody," Chip was saying. "We're going to race out to the buoy and back." He pointed to a blue metal buoy bobbing some distance out in the harbor. "Anyone who beats me back to the beach gets a hundred grand! Good luck. And may the best man win!"

"Don't worry," said Denny, glaring at Chip. "I will."

Soon we were all in the water, seated in our kayaks—I, for one, filled with newfound confidence. A confidence that quickly faded once Chip shouted, "On your mark, get set, *go!*"

Paddling had been so much easier in the air than it was in the water. Gaak. It was like trying to plow through molasses.

Everyone shot out in front me.

True, Cory and Bree were abysmally slow, but compared to me, they were speed demons.

Denny quickly gained the lead, his paddle spinning like a windmill in a tornado. But soon, muscles straining, Chip caught up with him. Then, in a moment that had to go down in the annals of dirty fighting, he swiped at Denny's paddle, sending it flying into the water.

Letting out a string of curses, Denny managed to retrieve his paddle. But not fast enough to catch up with Chip, who had gained a sizable lead.

It looked like Chip was a shoo-in to win when Cassidy caught up with him. They went at it neck and neck for a while, Cassidy edging into the lead, but then, in a final burst of energy, Chip zipped past her, first to arrive back on shore.

Mind you, I saw none of this exciting photo finish, because while the others were paddling back to the beach, I still hadn't even come close to the buoy.

Versel filled me in on Cassidy's almost-win once I was back on land, certain Cassidy had let her dad win.

"Otherwise," she'd sighed, "there would've been hell to pay."

Now, still straggling toward the buoy, I heard Chip whoop in victory.

Then I heard him shout, "Is Jaine still in the water? Somebody go out and get her."

Soon Jason had paddled his way out to me, and after hitching my kayak to his, towed me back in.

All in all, a most humiliating experience.

Joining the others, I saw Denny glowering as Chip cried, "Iron Man scores again!"

"Only because you cheated," Denny said.

"No way did I cheat," Chip had the audacity to lie. "I won fair and square."

"You did too cheat! I saw you!" were the words I would've uttered if I hadn't been afraid of losing my twenty-thousand-dollar paycheck.

Then Chip turned his unwelcome attention to me.

"My God, Jaine, I've seen toddlers paddle faster than you! You've got to be the world's slowest kayaker. We should have your paddle bronzed for posterity."

"Yeah, we should," I said.

And I knew exactly where I'd shove it.

Chapter Nine

I may have been the slowest kayaker in the history of kayaking, but I'd worked up quite an appetite paddling those few measly feet in the water.

By the time we'd changed back to our clothes in the Kayak Adventures locker room and taken a limo to Chip's favorite winery for lunch, I was ready to eat the tablecloth.

We were seated outside on the patio, Chip at the head of the table, Versel at the foot.

Denny and I nabbed seats next to Versel, both of us determined to sit as far as possible from our not-so-genial host, who at the moment was berating Cory for his lackluster performance in the kayak race.

"For crying out loud, Cory. You're almost as bad as Jaine."

On the limo ride, Chip had subjected me to a mind-numbing lecture on kayaking techniques, yammering gobbledygook about active blades, engaging my core, and torso rotation. (Or tire rotation; I wasn't really listening.)

The man was way too in love with the sound of his own voice.

Meanwhile, here on the patio, the view was breathtaking—a panoramic vista of the winery's meticulously manicured vineyard.

But, I must confess, I wasn't paying much attention to those grapes ripening on the vine, eager instead to check out the menu.

I'd been hoping for a nice juicy burger and fries but was met with a list of frou-frou offerings that left my taste buds asking, *What the what? Are we actually supposed to eat this stuff?*

For a whopping $150 a person, we'd each get four courses, plus wines to go with each course.

The disappointing menu included carrot hummus, wild mushroom mousse on toasted brioche, and rabbit tortellini.

(Heck, I love pasta, but no way was I about to eat a bunny rabbit.)

Oh, well. At least I could fill up on bread. But when I looked around for a bread basket, I saw not a hint of my beloved carbs anywhere.

Soon a waiter was bringing us our first course—a tiny dollop of carrot hummus marooned in the center of a very large plate.

An accompanying sommelier was pouring wine.

"Fill 'er up!" Denny demanded, holding out his glass, on the road to getting soused. "And bring another bottle!"

I stared down at my plate in dismay. It was the first time I'd ever been served hummus without pita bread. What sort of carbo-hating joint was this anyway?

"Would it be possible to get some bread?" I asked our waiter, a skinny guy with a pinched face and a "kiss my corkscrew" attitude.

"Sorry, ma'am," he said, eyeing me like I was a cockroach who'd just wandered in from a greasy-spoon diner. "We don't serve bread here at Snooty Haven Estates Winery."

Okay, it wasn't really called Snooty Haven Estates. But it should have been.

"Here, hon," Versel said, reaching into her tote. "Have a pretzel."

I grabbed it eagerly.

"The lady asked for bread," Denny snapped at the waiter. "Bring her some."

"But we don't serve bread, sir."

"You got that mushroom glop on brioche. Bring us brioche. Two loaves."

"And some butter," Cory added.

My heroes!

"A toast," Denny said, raising his wineglass when our waiter had stalked off in a huff. "To Chip—a lying, conniving SOB. I'll never forget the day we met. But I'm sure trying."

"Right back at you," Chip smirked. "Too bad you didn't finish first in the race. You could've used that 100K now that you're about to be unemployed."

"Unemployed?" Versel asked, shocked. "What are you talking about?"

"Your prince of a brother fired me last night," Denny explained.

"Chip, how could you?" Versel cried.

"Last I looked, VD, I was the one running this company, not you. So keep your opinions, and your goddamn pretzels, to yourself."

For a minute I thought Versel was going to hurl her bag of pretzels clear across the table at Chip, but unfortunately, that didn't happen.

By now, I'd long since inhaled my dollop of hummus and was overjoyed when our snootburger waiter showed up with two baskets of brioche and several ramekins of butter.

"For the lady," the waiter said, glaring at me.

Somehow I managed to rein in my impulse to bop him

over the head with my hummus plate. Instead, I grabbed a piece of bread.

So did Cory.

"Can somebody please pass me the butter?" he asked.

"Butter?" Chip shook his head in disgust. "The last thing you need is butter. Not with that pot belly of yours. No wonder you can't kayak worth a damn. Why can't you be more like your sister?"

Cory's jaw was clenched, his face an unsettling shade of red. Apparently, the last straw had just fallen on this camel's back.

"Why can't *you* be a decent human being?" he exploded. "Iron Man? Hah! More like Lyin' Man. Everybody saw you knock Denny's paddle into the water."

"That's not true," Avery piped up in defense of her fiancé. "I saw no such thing."

"Probably because you were too busy appraising your ring," Cory snapped at his future stepmom.

"Don't get too attached to it, hon," Denny said. "He'll probably sue you for it in the divorce settlement."

Avery sat ramrod straight in her chair.

"If you think I'm marrying Chip for his money, you're sadly mistaken," she said, icicles dripping from each syllable.

"Why else would you marry the miserable old bastard?" Cory asked.

"Who the hell do you think you are," Chip exploded, "talking about me like that?"

"I'm your son, not your whipping boy," Cory shouted right back at him. "You're a sorry excuse for a father, and if you ask me, the world would be a better place without you. Now would somebody pass me the goddamn butter?"

"Here you go, honey," Bree said, with a sly grin. Clearly she'd loved every moment of this battle royale.

By now all the other well-heeled winos on the patio were looking over at our table, either horrified or titillated by the dramatic exchange they'd just witnessed.

It was far more filling than the weensy food portions, that's for sure.

A silence descended on our table as we polished off the rest of our meager meal, abetted by several extra bottles of wine Denny had ordered.

Just as we were being served dessert—tarte tatins the size of a quarter—a handsome young guy in jeans and a tight-fitting tee approached our table, a motorcycle helmet tucked under his arm.

"Got your text, babe," he said to Cassidy. "Ready to go?"

"Who is this guy," Chip asked, "and what is he talking about?"

"This is my friend Michael, and he's taking me back to Los Angeles. I've had it up to here with all the negative energy on this trip. Aunt Versel, would you mind packing my things? I'll pick them up back in town."

"Of course, sweetheart."

Cassidy got up from the table and walked off with her motorcycle honey, his arm tight around her waist.

I was sitting there, wishing that I, too, could get the hell out of Dodge, when our snootburger waiter showed up and handed Chip the check.

"Nice work, Denny," Chip said, looking it over. "You added about $600 of extra wine charges to the bill."

I shuddered to think what it added up to.

And I was about to find out, because just then Chip tossed me the bill—for an eyepopping $1,379!

"You think I didn't notice your cat scratching my tapestry?" he said. "Of course I did. Nothing gets by me, Jaine. Which means you owe me twenty-five grand to replace the tapestry."

"Twenty-five thousand dollars?" I practically shrieked.

"If I deduct the twenty thousand I'm paying you for the book, you still owe me five grand. Plus a hundred bucks for the bathing suit."

OMG. If he was using my salary to buy a new rug, that meant I'd be writing his stupid book for free.

"Anyhow," Chip was saying, "you can start repaying me by picking up the tab for lunch."

No wonder he kept silent while Denny was ordering those extra bottles of wine. He knew all along he'd be saddling me with the bill.

I took out my credit card and handed it to our waiter, who could barely contain his glee as I gulped in dismay.

I prayed my credit card would be declined, but those traitors at MasterCard let the charge go through, eager, no doubt, to receive the ensuing interest payments. With a sigh as deep as the Grand Canyon, I hastily scribbled my signature, cursing the day I ever answered the ad for this damn job.

And PS. I didn't even get the chance to stiff our waiter, since the service charge was already added in. But I drew a frowny face on the bill.

That had to have stung, right?

Chapter Ten

Back on the train, I stormed into my cabin, oozing fury.
Thank goodness I wouldn't have to lay eyes on Chip
until happy hour at six.

Iron Man had decreed that we'd all retreat to our cabins
until then, so he could have a power nap. (It never even
occurred to him that the rest of us might want to get together without him.)

I was in my cabin, reeling at the thought of that twenty-
five-thousand-dollar tapestry bill—and chowing down on
some brioche I'd stolen from Snooty Estates Winery—
when I heard someone knock on my door.

It was Sean, with Prozac in his arms.

"Hi," he said, treating me to a special appearance of his
laugh lines. "I just stopped by to drop off your cat."

"Thanks so much for watching her. I hope she wasn't
too much trouble."

"Not at all. She was a total sweetheart."

Pro gazed up at him adoringly.

I think I'm in love.

"So how was your day?" Sean asked.

Was it my imagination, or did he seem reluctant to
leave? Could it be that he was a wee bit interested in me?

"An utter nightmare," I replied. "That 'sweetheart' in your arms just cost me twenty-five thousand dollars."

"Wow! How did that happen?"

"She clawed a few threads from Chip's tapestry in the parlor car."

A proud meow from Pro.

It looks so much better now!

"And Chip expects me to buy him a new one."

Sean shook his head in disbelief.

"And I thought having to buy him a new tablecloth was bad."

"What a ghastly guy," I fumed. "He cheats at kayaking and seems to get his jollies torturing poor Cory."

"Yeah, I've seen how he treats Cory. And he's not all that great with his staff, either. Fortunately, this is just a one-time assignment. I'd never work for him again."

Oh, how I wished I didn't have to, thinking of my twenty-thousand-dollar paycheck winging its way back into Chip's coffers.

"I'd better get going," Sean said, handing Prozac back to me.

Her cue to start yowling.

Wait! No! I wanna stay with Sean a little longer. Say, for the next year or two?

"That's enough, young lady," I said, shooting her a death ray glare.

That cat knows when she's in deep doo-doo with me, so she didn't treat us to an aria of wailing as she normally would, just a small whimper of protest as I plopped her down on the cabin's window seat.

"See you at dinner," Sean said to me. Then, to Pro: "Bye, cutie!"

She gazed up at him like a lap dancer at a billionaire's bachelor party.

Ciao for now, lover boy.

The minute he left, I whirled on Pro.

"Thanks to you, I owe Chip twenty-five grand! And I have to write his damn book for free. I am *thisclose* to trading you in for a houseplant!"

A plaintive meow, as she tried her best to look contrite.

You know what would make you feel better? Scratching my back for the next twenty minutes.

Actually, I knew from experience that she was right. Scratching her silky fur would make me feel better. But I wasn't about to reward her bad behavior.

Instead, I flopped down on the bed to stew over the events of my disastrous day. How could I possibly get the money to pay Chip? I'd have to cash out my CD, which I was saving for a rainy day and/or a pilgrimage to the Museum of Ice Cream in Austin, Texas.

I was in the middle of several rather satisfying revenge fantasies—slipping a banana peel on Chip's treadmill, writing a book filled with typos and grammatical errors (not that he'd ever notice), spiking his Iron Man Martini with a healthy dose of castor oil—when it suddenly occurred to me:

What if the tapestry was a fake? What if Chip bought it for ninety-nine bucks on Overstock.com? I wouldn't put it past him. Chip was a liar and a cheat, exactly the kind of guy who'd try to bilk twenty-five grand out of an innocent freelance writer.

With that, I jumped out of bed.

I didn't care if Chip was in the middle of his stupid power nap. I was going to march to his cabin and demand proof that his tapestry was really worth twenty-five grand.

Filled with righteous indignation, I looked out my cabin

door, only to see Sean leaving Chip's room and hustling off to the kitchen. I wanted to ask him what sort of mood Chip was in, but by the time I stepped out into the corridor, he was gone. Oh, well. I'd find out soon enough, I thought, as I stomped over to Chip's cabin.

Once I got his to his door, however, I was suddenly paralyzed.

As much as I wanted to, I couldn't bring myself to knock.

Remembering how Chip had screamed at his employee on the phone during my interview at his mansion, I chickened out, afraid to unleash Chip's volcanic temper.

Meekly, I retreated to my cabin, my righteous indignation having floated off into the ether.

I'd confront him later, after dinner and a fortifying glass of wine or three.

Exhausted from the stress of the day, I collapsed onto my daybed, where I promptly proceeded to conk out.

When I woke up, the train had started up again, heading back to L.A. It was after six, and I was late for happy hour. Jumping out of bed, I splashed some water on my face, corralled my curls into a scrunchy, and added a dash of lipstick (just in case I ran into Sean).

Leaving Prozac snoring full blast, I made my way to the parlor car.

I cringed at the thought of seeing Chip behind the bar whipping up his obnoxious martinis, but when I got there, he was nowhere in sight. The rest of the gang were all there. But not Iron Man.

The others were laughing and chatting among themselves, Denny acting as bartender.

Gone was the negative vibe Cassidy had been so eager to escape. Apparently life was a lot more fun without Iron Man around.

The only one who seemed to miss Chip was his bride-to-be, Avery, whose face fell when she saw it was me and not Chip coming into the parlor car.

But I didn't mind. I was just happy to be in a Chip-free zone. And my mood got even brighter when I saw a plate of puff pastry hors d'oeuvres on the bar. Just as I was reaching for one, Avery said, "Jaine, as long as you're up, would you mind going to Chip's cabin to see what's keeping him?"

I wasn't thrilled at the prospect, but surely he'd be through napping by now. And I was certain he wouldn't want to miss happy hour.

Chomping on my puff pastry (stuffed with pine nuts and feta cheese), I returned to Chip's cabin and knocked on his door.

No answer.

I knocked again. Still no answer.

Finally, praying I wouldn't catch him strutting around in his undies, I pushed open the door.

The cabin was twice the size of mine, with a large mahogany bed, over which hung a plaque reading WORLD'S BEST LOVER.

(World's best lover? The man's ego knew no bounds!)

But I wasn't interested in the furnishings, or Chip's monumental ego—my eyes riveted on Chip himself, who was definitely not strutting around in his undies.

Instead, he was lying on his bed, a WORLD'S BEST DAD throw pillow covering his face.

I suddenly felt more than a tad uneasy.

Was it possible Chip slept with a pillow over his head?

"Chip?" I called out.

No reply.

Something wasn't right about this.

I tiptoed over to the bed and lifted the pillow from Chip's face, then gasped to see his eyes wide open, unblinking.

"Chip?" I said, hoping beyond hope that he was a guy who liked to power nap with his eyes open.

But again, I was met with silence.

Finally I put my hand under his nose to see if he was breathing.

Nada.

By now there was no denying it. Chip Miller was dead. It was possible he'd simply died in his sleep.

But not likely. Not likely at all.

I'd bet my bottom Pop-Tart he'd been smothered to death with a WORLD'S BEST DAD throw pillow.

Chapter Eleven

"Chip's dead!" I cried, racing into the parlor car. Notice how I tactfully refrained from adding that, in my humble op, he'd been bumped off with a WORLD'S BEST DAD throw pillow.

"Omigod!" Avery jumped up and raced out of the parlor car, Aunt Versel on her heels. Somewhat reluctantly putting down their drinks, Cory and Bree headed out after them.

Only Denny remained behind, sipping from a martini.

"You sure he's really dead?" he asked.

"Positive. Unless he's mastered the art of napping without breathing."

Denny shot me a sly smile.

"Couldn't have happened to a more deserving guy."

With that, he took another slug of his martini, while I, as I often do in times of stress, headed straight for the chow—grabbing a salami roll-up from the hors d'oeuvres at the bar.

I'd just popped it in my mouth when I realized the train wasn't moving. Looking out the window, I saw we were back at Union Station in L.A.

Someone had called 911, and the police had shown up, their footsteps thumping in the sleeper car.

"Everybody return to your cabins," I heard one of them call out.

The next thing I knew, two cops had joined me and Denny in the parlor car, muscular guys whose faces were a blur in my mind, discombobulated as I was from my recent close encounter with a corpse.

"Please return to your cabin, sir," one of them instructed Denny.

"Not you," he added, as I got up to leave. "You stay here. You're Jaine Austen, right? The one who found the body?"

I nodded my head, my mouth too full of salami to reply.

"Can you tell us what happened?"

Swallowing my salami, I managed a recap of how I'd gone to check up on Chip and found him dead beneath his WORLD'S BEST DAD throw pillow.

One of them took notes as I spoke, and when I was through, they asked me for my contact info and said I was free to go.

My, that was a lot less painful than I'd expected.

After giving them my address and phone number, I hurried back to my cabin, where I found Prozac hard at work clawing the velvet coverlet I'd stowed away under my bed. Somehow the little devil had managed to pull open the storage drawer.

Oh, hell. Yet another charge on my rapidly growing bill.

"Stop that right now!" I commanded. "We're leaving."

A petulant meow.

But I haven't finished clawing this valuable coverlet to ribbons.

I snatched her from the coverlet and put her in her carrier, luring her there with a hunk of salami I'd purloined from the bar.

The second she'd inhaled it, she started yowling for more. But I didn't care. She could yowl all she wanted. Nothing was going to distract me from getting off this cursed train.

I hurled my belongings into my suitcase and, minutes later, was sprinting out to the corridor, where I smelled the heavenly aroma of something yummy cooking. Mario had undoubtedly started preparing dinner before Chip's body had been discovered. I had a momentary pang of regret at the thought of missing out on what was sure to have been an excellent meal. If last night was any indication, Mario was a culinary whiz.

But for once in my life my taste buds were overruled by my desire to flee the train. I did not pop into the kitchen to grab a sample of whatever Mario had been whipping up.

Instead I raced for the stairs leading to the platform.

Sean was standing there, as he'd been when I first showed up at the Iron Man Express yesterday. (Had it been only a day since I boarded? It felt like centuries!)

This time Sean was there to say goodbye.

"It was fun," he said, with a most appealing grin. "Not the trip, or the murder, of course. But getting to meet you."

I felt my heart flutter just a tad.

"Likewise," I managed to say.

He looked like he was on the verge of saying something else.

Please, let him ask me out! I prayed to the gods above.

But my prayers were not about to be answered.

All I got was a polite, "Take care."

I swallowed my disappointment and started walking away.

"Bye, sweetie!" he called out.

I beamed with pleasure.

Until I turned around and realized he'd been waving at Prozac.

From her cage, a triumphant meow.

I knew all along he liked me better than you!

So much for romance on the rails.

You've Got Mail!

To: Jausten
From: Shoptillyoudrop
Subject: Buzzing with Excitement

Everyone at Tampa Vistas is abuzz with excitement about the costume party. Darling centenarian Mildred Kimble is coming as Shirley Temple. And Edna Lindstrom and Nick Roulakis have teamed up and are coming as Fred and Ethel Mertz from *I Love Lucy*. Isn't that clever? Which got me to thinking that Daddy and I should team up, too. He can wear a tuxedo and come as The Great Gatsby to match my flapper costume. Won't that be fun?

XOXO,
Mom

To: Jausten
From: DaddyO
Subject: Good Grief!

Good grief, Lambchop! Now Mom wants me to wear a tuxedo to the costume party. No way am I wearing an uncomfortable tux all night, with a cummerbund digging at my waist. I'm going as Hugh Hefner in my robe and pajamas, and that's final!

Oops. Someone's at the door. Gotta run.
Love 'n snuggles from
Daddy

To: Jausten
From: Shoptillyoudrop
Subject: Off the Deep End!

Your daddy has gone off the deep end. No time to explain now. Will write more later.

XOXO,
Mom

To: Jausten
From: DaddyO
Subject: Fantastic News!

Fantastic news, Lambchop!

That was the UPS guy at the door just now with a package from the estate of my late Uncle John. You never got to meet him, but he was my favorite uncle. Such a funny man! Every year at Thanksgiving, he used to take out his glass eye, put it in my mashed potatoes, and say, "Here's looking at you, kid."

Anyhow, the package from Uncle John was full of family memorabilia. I was looking through an old photo album when I came across an autographed photo of Elvis Presley with the inscription: *To Uncle John from your ever-lovin' nephew, Elvis.*

Do you know what that means, Lambchop? Elvis Presley was my cousin! Imagine being related to Elvis the Pelvis—and Henry VIII!

Naturally, now that I know about my heritage, I've made up my mind to dump Hugh Hefner and come to the costume party as Elvis. So much more fun than the Battle-Axe's boring old Betsy Ross.

I can't wait to see her seethe with envy.

Love 'n hugs from your
Genetically blessed
Daddy

P.S. I don't mind telling you I'm more than a little disappointed in your mom. She insists that I can't possibly be related to Elvis, that Uncle John probably bought the photo at a yard sale. But that makes no sense whatsoever. Who in their right mind would sell an autographed photo of Elvis Presley at a yard sale? That picture's got to be worth a fortune.

To: Jausten
From: Shoptillyoudrop
Subject: No Possible Way!

I suppose Daddy's told you about the Elvis photo. And how he's convinced he's Elvis's cousin (not to mention a direct descendant of Henry VIII!). I swear, that man has been watching way too many episodes of *Finding Your Roots*.

There's no possible way Daddy can be related to Elvis. His whole family comes from Massachusetts; there's not a southern bone in his body. Uncle John probably picked up the photo at a yard sale and forged the autograph himself.

The man was more than a little off his rocker. Would you believe he'd actually take out his glass eye at the dinner table and put it in Daddy's mashed potatoes?

But Daddy's convinced the picture is genuine.

Oh, Lord. He's online right now, ordering an Elvis costume to wear to the party.

Time to soothe my fraying nerves with some fudge.

XOXO,
Mom

To: Jausten
From: DaddyO
Subject: The Transformation Begins!

The transformation begins, Lambchop! I just ordered an Elvis outfit to wear to the costume party, along with a wig and a Lady Elvis outfit for Mom.

Later, alligator!
Daddy

To: Jausten
From: Shoptillyoudrop

Now Daddy expects me to go to the costume party as Lady Elvis! He went ahead and ordered a costume for me, without even asking. Well, he's going to be sending it right back. Because I have no intention of wearing it. I'm going in my cute little flapper dress and plan to spend the evening steering clear of Daddy. I just hope his Elvis costume isn't too over the top and that he'll blend in with the rest of the crowd.

XOXO,
Mom

To: Jausten
From: DaddyO
Subject: Grand Entrance

Guess what, Lambchop? I thought of a terrific way to stand out from the crowd at the costume party. I'm getting a body microphone so that I can not only show up dressed as Elvis, I can make my grand entrance singing "You Ain't Nothing But a Hound Dog."

Can't wait to see the expression on La Pinkus's face when I snatch first prize out from under her!

Love 'n stuff from
Daddy

Chapter Twelve

I woke up the next morning, thrilled to be back on terra firma, snug in bed with Prozac clawing my chest for her breakfast, the remains of Chinese takeout I'd ordered the night before on my night table.

I know you're supposed to be sorry when someone dies, but in Chip's case, I was willing to make an exception. Working for the guy would have been a nightmare. Cory was right when he said the world would be a better place without him. My world certainly was.

And so I jumped out of bed with a spring in my step, joy in my heart, and a few stray wonton noodles in my hair.

After fixing Pro her breakfast, I nuked myself some coffee and my usual cinnamon raisin bagel slathered with butter and strawberry jam.

Settling down on my sofa, I checked my parents' emails, trying to decide which was more mind-boggling—the fact that Daddy thought he was Elvis's cousin or that Uncle John used to toss his glass eye in Daddy's mashed potatoes.

Clearly, ours was a nut-bearing family tree.

I'd just started to dig into my CRB when I heard a knock on my front door.

I opened it to find a man and a woman standing at my

doorstep. Due to my amazing powers of perception, I knew right away they were detectives.

(And also because they showed me their badges.)

The man, Detective H. Banuelos, was stocky and barrel-chested. The woman, Detective L. LaMott, was stocky and flat-chested. Both wore shiny polyester suits and had the weary-eyed look of cops who'd seen a lot of stuff they wished they hadn't.

"Ms. Austen?" LaMott said.

I nodded.

"We're here to ask you some follow-up questions regarding the death of Chip Miller."

"Of course. Come in and have a seat," I said, brushing bagel crumbs from the sofa. "I'll just clear this stuff away."

I grabbed my bagel and toted it to the kitchen, scarfing down a quick bite en route.

When I returned to join the detectives, Prozac had wandered into the living room and hurled herself at Banuelos's ankles, rubbing up against them with wild abandon.

Hey there, officer! Wanna pet me for the next hour or so?

"Stop that, Pro!" I said, snatching her away from the detective, who looked none too pleased as he brushed cat hairs from his trousers.

"So how can I help you?" I asked, sitting across from them in my overstuffed chintz armchair, wishing I were wearing something more confidence-inspiring than my coffee-stained chenille bathrobe.

"According to the police report," LaMott said, "you were the one who found Mr. Miller's body."

"That's right. Chip hadn't shown up for happy hour, so his fiancée asked me to check on him in his cabin. When I got there, I found him lying on the bed with a throw pillow over his face.

"At first I thought maybe he was asleep, but when I

lifted the pillow and checked his breathing, I realized he was dead, smothered by the throw pillow."

"It's true Mr. Miller was smothered to death," Banuelos said. "But how did you know that? How did you know he hadn't died of a heart attack?"

Was it because you were the one who smothered him? were the unspoken words that hung like a thundercloud over my living room.

Oh, hell. They thought I was the killer! I cursed myself for ever touching that damn throw pillow. Now my DNA was all over the murder weapon.

"Chip was a pretty nasty guy," I hastened to defend myself. "The kind of guy who made enemies. I just assumed he'd been killed."

"Exactly what was your relationship with the deceased?" asked LaMott.

"He'd hired me to ghostwrite an exercise guidebook."

"You? Write an exercise book?" she snickered in reply, not even bothering to hide her amusement as she gave my thighs the once-over.

Of all the nerve! First they practically accuse me of murder, and now this snark bite. So much for any future donations to the Police Athletic League.

"It seems Mr. Miller was billing you twenty-five thousand dollars to replace a tapestry your cat had damaged," Banuelos was saying.

Pro looked up, preening, from where she'd been giving herself a thorough gynecological exam.

I still think it looks much better now.

"Twenty-five thousand dollars is a lot of money," said LaMott. "Especially for a woman whose bathrobe has coffee stains from the Eisenhower administration."

Okay, she didn't really say the part about my bathrobe, but I knew she was thinking it.

"What are you implying? That I killed Chip to get out of paying him back?"

"Murders have been committed for a lot less than twenty-five thousand dollars."

I didn't like this line of questioning. Not one bit.

"Life must be so much easier for you," said Banuelos, "without that debt hanging over your head."

"Who says the charge isn't hanging over my head? For all I know, I'll still be billed for the tapestry."

"As you already pointed out, Mr. Miller was known to be a pretty nasty guy. Maybe you were hoping the rest of the family would go easy on you and drop the charge."

That's exactly what I'd been hoping.

But I wasn't about to give them the satisfaction of admitting it.

"I can assure you," I replied with an indignant huff, "I did not kill Chip Miller."

"Any idea who else might have done it?"

Absolutely! Cory, Bree, and Denny were my front-runners. I remembered how Denny stayed behind in the parlor car while the others raced to check on Chip. Maybe Denny didn't have to check—because he was the one who'd smothered him.

Normally I hate to throw people under the bus. But at that moment, it was either them or me.

"Cory Miller had a strained relationship with his dad, to put it mildly. Chip seemed to get a sadistic pleasure out of belittling him. They'd had a big blowup at lunch, with Cory essentially telling Chip that he wished he was dead. What's more, I'd overheard Cory's wife threatening to leave him unless he did something about his dad and got a promotion at work. And Chip had just fired Denny, his right-hand man, who was furious about getting dumped."

"Did you happen to see any of them enter Mr. Miller's cabin the afternoon of the murder?"

"No," I admitted.

"Did you see anyone else enter Mr. Miller's cabin?"

I suddenly remembered seeing Sean coming out of Chip's cabin. Was it possible he'd been there to bump him off?

My judgment may have been a bit clouded because of my raging warmies for the guy, but I couldn't believe Sean was the killer. He'd never even met Chip before the trip. True, Chip was charging him for a new tablecloth, but that was hardly a motive for murder.

"No, I didn't see anyone go into Chip's cabin."

Technically the truth. I saw Sean *leave* the cabin, but I never actually saw him go in.

At long last, the detectives got up to go.

"Thanks for your time," said Banuelos. "We'll be in touch if we need to ask any more questions."

Lord, I hoped not.

"Enjoy your bagel," added LaMott, "and in the future, try not to touch any more murder weapons at the scene of a crime."

After showing them out, I slumped down on my sofa in a deep funk.

Just like that, I'd gone from freelance writer to murder suspect. For all I knew, the prime suspect.

I was so upset, I couldn't even finish my bagel.

Okay, I finished it, but it tasted like cardboard in my mouth.

I was just heading to the kitchen to nuke myself another—What can I say? I'm a stress eater—when Lance showed up.

He sailed into my apartment in a tank top and cutoffs, his blond curls looking extra bouncy.

"Welcome home, sweetie!" he cried, following me as I

headed back to the kitchen. "How'd everything go on the train trip?"

"My boss got killed, and the cops think I did it."

"That's nice," he said, helping himself to half of the bagel I'd just buttered.

Arggh. The guy hadn't heard a word I said. Which often happens when he's caught up in his own adventures in Lance-land.

"Fabulous news! I've been invited to a cocktail party at the Empire Club."

I remembered the snooty social club he'd been angling to join, where his boss at Neiman's was a member.

"How did you manage to snag an invitation?"

"I just happened to mention to Kelvin, my boss, that I'm best friends with European royalty."

"What European royalty? Count Chocula?"

"Contessa Anastasia Magdalena of Romania," he said, ignoring my attempt at sarcasm. "Once Kelvin found out we were *thisclose*, he invited me to the party as his guest and insisted I bring her along."

"But you don't know any countesses from Romania."

"That's where you come in, sweetie. I want *you* to play the part of the contessa."

He beamed at me like he'd just chosen me to star on Broadway.

"What the what?!"

"No need to thank me, hon. I know you'll be terrific."

"I won't be terrific because I'm not going to do it. For starters, I don't speak a word of Romanian."

"Not a problem. I've already told them you don't speak English, so you won't have to say a word. All you have to do is stand around looking regal. Which sounds like Mission Impossible, I know, but I'm up for the challenge. You'll be my own Eliza Doolittle. I'll have you transformed from guttersnipe to countess before you can say, 'The rain in Spain stays mainly in the plain.' "

"Forget it, Henry Higgins. No way am I letting you do a makeover on me."

"But, Jaine—"

"Not a chance!" I said, holding out my palm to cut off any further discussion. "I refuse to have you curling my lashes and straightening my hair, and squishing my guts into a torture chamber of Spanx. And absolutely nothing you say will get me to me change my mind."

"How about a year's subscription to the Brownie of the Month Club?"

I did not hesitate, not for a moment, before I replied:

"When do we start?"

Okay, so I sold my soul for a year's worth of brownies.

At the time, it seemed worth it.

(In my defense, March, June, and October came with double crème chocolate frosting.)

Chapter Thirteen

After Lance left, I slumped down on my sofa in a funk. How quickly the day had gone from swell to hell. The sun seemed duller, the clouds grayer. Even the birds, whose chirps seemed so merry when I woke up, now sounded like tiny jackhammers in my ear.

Not only was I a prime murder suspect, I still had that dratted twenty-five-thousand-dollar tapestry bill hanging over my head. And wouldn't you know? I had absolutely zero writing assignments lined up. I could practically hear my checking account breathing its last gasp.

I called my regular clients (the friendly folks at Toilet-masters Plumbers, Tip Top Dry Cleaners, and Fiedler on the Roof Roofers), but nobody had any work for me. So I hopped over to my computer and started sending my résumé to on-line job postings, applying for any copywriting gig listed.

Apparently copywriting had gone the way of the dodo bird, since I found only three jobs I was even remotely qualified for.

I considered faking it and pretending to be a tech writer (there were at least twenty ads for those), but given the fact that it took me months to figure out how to stream a movie on Roku, I decided that little ploy was bound to blow up in my face.

Refusing to let the day be a total washout, I spent the rest of the afternoon giving my apartment a thorough cleaning.

Okay, I spent the rest of the afternoon in bed watching old movies with Pro and a bag of Oreos.

Actually, a very wise decision. Chocolate is nature's antidepressant, you know. By the time I went to bed that night, I was filled with renewed hope, determined to hunt down Chip's killer and clear my name—and to get out from under that ghastly tapestry bill.

And the one person who could help me with both was Versel Rush.

The next morning, I tooled over to Chip's mansion to pay a condolence call on Versel, toting a homemade spaghetti pie.

Not homemade by me, of course, but by my local supermarket's deli department.

Hoping for some alone time with Versel and fearing the house might be filled with mourners, I was happy to note there were no cars parked in the driveway when I pulled up.

I rang the bell and soon heard footsteps shuffling in the grand foyer.

The door opened, and Versel stood there in a chenille bathrobe much like my own, her gray hair tousled, her cheeks creased with pillowcase wrinkles.

"Jaine, honey. How nice to see you! Excuse the way I look," she said, suppressing a yawn. "I just woke up a little while ago. Come on in. I was about to pour myself some coffee."

She waved me in, and I followed as she led me to the mansion's spacious kitchen at the rear of the house.

Aside from a dishwasher and stainless steel fridge, the room looked like it hadn't been updated since the house was built sometime, I was guessing, in the 1930s. It still had the original sink and cabinetry. And instead of a monster island, a homey farmhouse table and chairs sat in the middle of the room.

"Have a seat while I get us some coffee," she said, bustling around, pouring coffee from an old-fashioned percolator into thick ceramic mugs.

"Chip always woke me up at the crack of dawn. What a luxury to be able to sleep in.

"Here you go," she said, bringing our mugs to the table. "Cream or sugar?"

"Both," I replied.

"Me, too."

She headed for the refrigerator and soon was back with real cream. What a treat!

(If there's one thing that ought to be abolished by law, it's coffee with skim milk.)

"I brought you something," I said, when we were sitting catty-corner across from each other at the kitchen table. "Spaghetti pie."

I reached into the supermarket shopping bag I'd been carrying and pulled out a container of spaghetti baked with tomato sauce and gooey cheese.

"Oh my, this looks delicious. But spaghetti pie for breakfast?" Then she broke out in a grin. "What a great idea!"

After grabbing plates and silverware, she doled out generous chunks of the carbo-cheesy concoction.

"So how are you holding up?" I asked.

"I'm okay," she sighed. "Chip was a pain in the fanny to live with, but I've got to admit I'm going to miss him. We both went through some pretty tough times growing up, with no money and parents who hated each other. Chip watched over me back then. And when my deadbeat husband, the ever-unreliable Herbert Rush, died and left me saddled with debts, Chip took me in and gave me a place to live. I know he seemed impossible, and he was impossible most of the time, but underneath it all, he loved me. And I loved him.

"Oh, dear. I can't believe I'm getting weepy," she said, wiping a tear from her eye with the sleeve of her bathrobe.

"But enough about me." She managed a weak smile. "How are you doing?"

"Not so good," I confessed, telling her about my visit from Detectives Banuelos and LaMott and how they suspected me of being the killer.

"Not only did I touch the murder weapon, but they think I might have killed Chip to get out of paying that twenty-five-thousand-dollar tapestry bill."

"That's absurd," Versel scoffed, indignant. "You're no killer."

"I don't suppose the tapestry was just a copy?" I asked.

"No, it was genuine."

Rats.

"But it doesn't need to be replaced. It can be repaired for only a few thousand dollars."

A few thousand dollars? That was still a big chunk of change to me.

"Don't worry," she added, seeing the worried look in my eyes. "The estate will pay for it. Not only that, I'm going to have the attorneys cut you a check for ten grand."

"Ten thousand dollars? But I only worked with Chip for a few hours."

"Consider it combat pay," she said with a wry smile.

Ten grand! What a boon to tide me over my dry work spell.

"Thank you so much!"

I wanted to get up and give her a great big hug, but that

would have meant letting go of my fork, so I blew her a kiss instead.

"I don't suppose you could possibly do me one more favor. As I said, I'm pretty sure the cops think I may have killed Chip. So I'd like to nose around and ask some questions on my own."

"You mean, like a private eye?"

"Part-time, semi-professional."

I told her about some of the murders I'd solved, action-packed adventures you can read about in the titles at the front of this book.

"Wow," she said when I was through. "A writer *and* a P.I. Not to mention a woman with impeccable taste in spaghetti pies. I'm impressed."

"I was hoping you'd be able to send me a contact list of everyone who was on board the Iron Man Express."

"No problem. I'll text it as soon as I'm through demolishing this pie."

"Including the staff," I added, remembering how I'd seen Sean leaving Chip's cabin the afternoon of the murder. I still couldn't believe a sweetie like Sean was the killer, but I needed to make sure.

"Speaking of the staff," Versel said, a mischievous gleam in her eye, "it seems you made quite an impression. A handsome young man called and asked me for your phone number."

Yay! Sean was interested in me after all!

"Yes, Mario seemed quite taken with you."

"Mario? The chef?" I asked, with a stab of disappointment. Sure, he was handsome in a swarthy, bodice-ripping, romance novel kind of way. But not my type. Not at all.

"How odd that he asked about me. We never even got a chance to talk."

"Apparently he noticed how much you liked his cooking and told me he's always been attracted to women with a hearty appetite."

I blushed at the memory of how I'd practically licked my dinner plate clean that night on the train.

"I hope you don't mind," Versel was saying, "but I gave him your number."

"No, that's fine," I said, secretly wishing my admirer had been Sean.

"Just one more question," I said. "I feel awkward even asking, but do you think there's any chance Cory could be the killer? After what he said at the winery, about the world being a better place without Chip? Do you think he was capable of murdering his own father?"

"Actually, Cory and Cassidy were both adopted. Chip's late wife was the one who pushed for it. She and Chip married back before he'd made all his money. She was a sweet woman, desperate for children. But it never happened for them, so she convinced Chip to adopt. Chip never really got into it."

So Cory had been adopted by a man who didn't want him. Very interesting.

"I suppose Cory stands to inherit a lot of money."

"The last I heard, the estate's being split three ways between me, Cory, and Cassidy. With a special fund set aside to build a statue of Chip at Muscle Factory headquarters."

Leave it to Chip to build a statue of himself, his ego living on from whatever circle of hell he'd been assigned to.

But all I could think about was Cory's hefty inheritance. Chip's house alone had to be worth millions. I found it more than easy to believe Cory was capable of knocking off his bully of an adoptive father, a man who took such pleasure in humiliating him, especially with all that money coming his way.

Now all I had to do was prove it.

Chapter Fourteen

As much as I wanted to pin the murder on Cory, I couldn't quite shake the memory of Sean scooting out of Chip's cabin.

Eager to erase him from my suspect list, I texted him, asking if he was free to meet up to talk about Chip's murder.

His reply came right away.

Sure. Tonight? 7:30? Paco's Tacos on Centinela Ave? (My favorite Mexican restaurant.)

Talk about your culinary soulmates. I love Paco's. I've eaten there so often they've practically named a burrito after me. I quickly texted back:

Great! See you then.

Wow. I'd been expecting a coffee date, not dinner. Surely that meant he was into me, right?

I tootled over to Paco's that night in a carefully curated outfit of skinny jeans and hip-camouflaging swing top. Sean was already seated when I came in.

He stood to greet me, wearing chinos and a tee.

It was the first time I'd seen him without his white steward jacket. And he was even cuter than I remembered—a tad on the scrawny side, but that's the way I like 'em. (Opposites attract and all that.)

His sandy hair, which had been neatly slicked back on

the train, was now loose and flopping onto his forehead. It was all I could do not to reach over and run my fingers through it.

"Good to see you, Jaine, " he said, flashing me a most endearing grin.

"You, too."

He had no idea how much I meant it.

"Hope you don't mind meeting here, but I was craving Mexican food."

"I love this place," I assured him. "I come here all the time."

"If you've never tried their chimichangas, they're the best in L.A."

Indeed they were. In fact, chimichangas were my go-to order at Paco's. But I'd made up my mind to order a salad that night. Sean had seen enough of me stuffing my face on the train. I was determined to order something ladylike— and not finish it.

"Actually, I was thinking of getting a tostada salad," I said.

"Are you sure? The chimichangas are fantastic."

"Okay," I said, as if I hadn't been inhaling them for years. "What the heck? I'll give them a shot."

At which point, our waiter approached our table. Unfortunately, he recognized me from the gazillion times I'd eaten there before.

"Chicken chimichangas with extra guac, right?" he said.

"I may have had them a few times," I confessed to Sean, blushing furiously.

So much for pawning myself off as a dainty eater.

But who cared? I was getting the chimichangas, just the thought of which made me salivate.

"And to drink?" asked our waiter.

"Margarita with salt," we both replied at the same time.

"Margaritas without salt are like fries without ketchup," said Sean.

I couldn't have agreed more. Clearly our taste buds had been separated at birth.

"Sorry I couldn't meet earlier today," Sean said when the waiter had gone. "I was working a catering job."

"Are you an actor?"

Scratch the surface of 99.9% of the waiters in L.A., and you'll find a budding actor.

"Heck, no," he laughed. "I'm a writer."

"That's great!"

And I meant it. I'd always wanted to match up with a writer.

"What do you write?"

I prayed he wouldn't say he was an aspiring screen-writer. That meant he'd be waiting tables for the rest of his life.

"I'm a freelance journalist."

"A journalist? Very impressive."

"But freelance work can be spotty."

"Tell me about it," I said, thinking of my anemic checking account.

"So I do the cater-waiter thing to make ends meet."

Before long our margaritas had shown up, and we were trading favorite author picks.

"I'm really into Tom Perrotta and Richard Russo," Sean said. "But I guess my all-time favorite is Anne Tyler."

"Omigosh, she's my fave, too!"

This was getting spooky. Not only were we culinary soulmates with a specialty in chimichangas; we were literary soulmates, too.

Soon we were talking about our favorite movies and TV shows.

"I'm hooked on home reno shows on HGTV," Sean said.

"You watch HGTV?"

"All the time."

It was official. He was either perfect for me. Or gay.

"I hate it when they tear down walls to build great rooms," he was saying. "I don't want people to see me in the kitchen making a mess when I cook."

"Me, neither!"

"Not that I do much cooking."

"Me, neither!"

"I actually use my oven to warm my jeans in the winter."

"Me, too!"

"And for storing unused pots and pans," he said.

"You must have a hidden camera in my kitchen. It's exactly what I do."

We were so busy chattering away I barely noticed when our waiter showed up with our chimichangas. Okay, I noticed. But I didn't dive into them as I usually do, caught up as we were in a heated exchange about pet peeves.

"Pineapple on a pizza?" Sean groaned. "Yuck!"

"Unthinkable!"

"And kale salads? The worst!"

"Like eating green cardboard!" I cried.

"And almond milk?"

"Ugh!"

"If God intended to make milk out of almonds, he would've given them udders."

"Amen to that," I said, as we clinked margarita glasses.

I was feeling such a connection with this cutie-pie journalist that I'd hardly made a dent in my chimichangas. Usually, by now I would have inhaled them both at the speed of light.

"So," he said, after we'd sung the praises of pepperoni

pizza and putting potato chips on sandwiches, "what was it you wanted to ask me about Chip's murder?"

Oh, foo. We were having such a wonderful time. I couldn't possibly ruin the magic and tell him I saw him leaving Chip's cabin. It was practically accusing him of murder. So, instead, I told him how the cops suspected me and asked him if he was aware of anyone going into Chip's cabin the afternoon of the murder.

"Just me."

I gulped in dismay, praying I wasn't about to hear a murder confession.

"I was there to drop off fresh towels. Chip insisted they be changed twice a day. I tiptoed in during his power nap, but I can assure you he was alive when I left."

It was possible my roaring crush on Sean was clouding my thinking, but it sure seemed like he was telling the truth.

And just like that, a weight lifted from my shoulders. My culinary soulmate and pineapple-on-pizza-hater was innocent!

"Did you see anyone else go in the cabin?" I asked.

"Nope. After I set the table for dinner, I went back to my own cabin to work on an article I'm writing. But if I hear of anything, I'll let you know. I can't believe the police suspect you of being the killer."

"Oh, it's nothing," I said, blowing off the very notion with a wave of my hand.

And in that moment, sitting across from my potential soulmate, the murder charge hanging over my head seemed to have vanished into the chimichanga-scented air.

We continued chatting, and when the check came, Sean insisted on paying.

Feminists around the world, forgive me, but I love it when a guy offers to pay. I find it incredibly sexy.

"No, really, we should split it," I said, hoping he wouldn't take the credit card I was holding out.

And he didn't.

"Absolutely not! This was my treat. In more ways than one," he added, zapping me with another grin.

Hello. That was a flirt-o-gram if I'd ever heard one. The guy was totally into me.

Or so I thought.

Because just then his cell phone rang.

He checked the screen and answered right away.

"Hi, hon," he said.

Hon? Who the heck was hon? His girlfriend, no doubt. Maybe even his wife!

"What's up? . . . Okay, I'll be right over.

"So sorry," he said, slapping some twenties down on the table. "I've gotta run. Great talking with you, Jaine."

And poof! He was gone, leaving me alone with my beans and rice and shattered dreams.

Oh, well. I should've known it was too good to be true.

For the first time ever, I'd finished only one of my chimichangas and had the waiter box the other.

True, I polished it off at the very first stoplight on my way home, but my heart wasn't in it.

Chapter Fifteen

When my phone rang the next morning, I indulged myself in a fleeting fantasy that it was Sean, that he'd broken up with his "hon," having fallen in love over chimichangas with yours truly.

No such luck.

It was Mario the chef.

"Versel Rush gave me your number," he said. "We didn't get a chance to talk on the train, but I felt an instant connection with you."

I remembered Versel telling me how Mario got off on my hearty appetite. He probably noticed my clean plate when Chip called him into the dining room to chew him out. Or maybe he was watching me eat from that window in the swinging door to the kitchen.

"Anyhow," he was saying, "I was hoping I could fix you dinner at my place tomorrow night."

Gosh, the guy really did like to watch me eat.

But I wasn't interested. Mario wasn't my type, too slickly handsome. And besides, I couldn't get Sean out of my mind.

"That's very sweet of you, but—"

"I'm making beef bourguignon with mashed potatoes, homemade French baguette, and profiteroles for dessert."

"What time should I be there?"

What can I say? He had me at "mashed potatoes."

I hung up, still wishing it had been Sean calling. But I had to stop obsessing about Sean and do something about that pesky murder rap jeopardizing my future.

My prime suspect was Cory. He had plenty of reasons to bump off his adoptive dad, not least of which was the boatload of money he stood to inherit. So I decided to pay him and his boobalicious wife Bree a visit, hoping to catch them unawares at home. I often like to pounce on my suspects without warning, giving them no time to polish their alibis.

Consulting Versel's contact list, I found their house in the Rancho Park neighborhood of West Los Angeles, a leafy enclave of modest mid-century homes.

Their Cape Cod was nice enough, but not even close to the splendor of Chip's mega-mansion.

After parking my Corolla, I headed up the front path with a bouquet of carnations I'd picked up at the supermarket. Inside I could hear the whir of a vacuum.

I rang the bell several times before the vacuuming finally stopped and a heavyset woman came to the door in joggers and baggy T-shirt with the words MERRY MAID SERVICE emblazoned across her chest.

"What is it?" she snapped, not the least bit merry.

And a great big hello to you, too, I was tempted to say. But instead went with, "Hi. I'm Jaine Austen, here to pay my condolences to Cory and Bree."

Like a bad actor reciting her lines, she said, "Mr. and Mrs. Miller are in mourning and much too upset to see visitors."

With that, she grabbed the carnations from my hand and slammed the door in my face.

Of all the nerve! I was sorely tempted to ring the door-bell and retrieve my carnations, but I forced myself to focus on the task at hand.

No way did I believe Cory and Bree were too upset to talk. Especially when, as I started to leave, I heard laughter and splashing coming from their backyard.

Looking around, I saw a path along the side of the house leading to the rear of the property. True, the path was quite narrow and overgrown with hedges. But on the plus side, there was no gate, nothing to stop me from heading out back.

Which turned out to be a lot easier said than done.

The hedges were old and dirty and covered with cob-webs.

I didn't know how Cory and Bree were spending their money, but it sure as heck wasn't on gardeners.

I was making my way along the narrow path, shoving branches out of my face and trying to steer clear of cob-webs, when suddenly a window sprang open and the maid who'd so rudely snatched away my carnations stuck her head out.

"What are you doing?" she hissed. "I already told you the Millers are too upset to see visitors. I'm calling the police!"

"Wait!" I frantically rummaged around in my bag for my wallet and pulled out a twenty-dollar bill.

"Here's twenty bucks," I said, thrusting it at her, "to forget you ever saw me."

"I don't know," she said, scratching her sweaty brow. "I got a pretty good memory."

With a sigh, I forked over another twenty.

"Okay," she said, "consider yourself forgotten. They're out back in the pool, celebrating like it's New Year's Eve.

After a death in the family. They should be ashamed of themselves," she added, tucking my twenties in her bra.

Then she shut the window, and I resumed my trek.

I'd almost reached the back of the house when I looked down and saw a humungous spider scooting up my pants. Yuck! It was brown and hairy and racing toward me with alarming speed.

Frantically, I brushed it away, but not without a high-pitched screech.

"What was that?" I heard Cory say.

Oh, hell! They'd heard me. I'd forked over forty bucks for nothing!

But then I heard Bree saying, "Probably Mrs. Engel next door giving herself a bikini wax."

Silently I blessed Mrs. Engel and at last made it to the back of the house, where I peered around the corner to see "the mourners" in a sparkling turquoise pool—clearly, they were paying their pool man a lot more than their gardener—lounging on rubber floats and sipping umbrella drinks, Cory's pot belly and Bree's boobs glistening in the midday sun.

So much for being too devastated for company.

"I'm so proud of you, honey," Bree was saying. "Everything worked out just the way we planned."

"I couldn't have done it without you, sweetie."

"To us!" Bree said, holding up her umbrella drink in a toast. "And to a bright new future!"

"You betcha!" said Cory, popping a maraschino cherry in his mouth.

I don't know about you, but that sounded to me like two killers celebrating a successful hit.

Anxious to avoid any more close encounters with an arachnid, I hurried back down the path to the front of the house, more convinced than ever that Cory was the killer, probably aided and abetted by his gold-digging wife.

When I finally emerged from those dratted hedges, shaking my head for errant spiders, I saw that the black crepe pants and silk shirt I'd chosen for my condolence call were smeared with dirt, the blouse having sustained a few fatal rips.

It was a brand-new blouse, too, half-off at Nordstrom.

But all in all a small price to pay for the damning chatter I'd just overheard.

Chapter Sixteen

If only I had some evidence linking the happy couple to Chip's murder.

And then I thought of Avery. Her cabin had been right next to Chip's. Was it possible she'd heard Cory and Bree in Chip's cabin on the afternoon of the murder?

I certainly didn't consider Avery a suspect. After all, she wasn't married to Chip yet. She hadn't had a chance to learn to despise him. And it seemed unlikely he'd left her anything in his will before they'd even tied the knot.

But I definitely needed to pay her a visit.

So as soon as I got back in my Corolla, I called and set up an appointment to see her the next day.

Eager to shed my filthy clothing, I hurried home and was trudging up the front path to my apartment when I ran into Lance, who was heading off for work, spiffed up in his designer togs.

"Omigod!" he said, plucking some leaves from my hair. "What happened to you? You look like you've just gone ten rounds with a leaf blower."

He shook his head in dismay.

"How I'm ever going to change you from guttersnipe to countess, I'll never know."

Then he brightened considerably.

"It's a daunting challenge, but I'm up for it! Be ready for a fashion fitting!" he cried as he scurried away.

I groaned at the thought of squeezing myself into the torture chamber outfit Lance would no doubt choose for me, then headed off to shower and change and have a brief memorial service for my silk blouse.

As I was to discover the next day, Avery Suzuki Tomkins Feinberg lived in a spectacular high-rise condo in Century City. She came to the door in a cashmere lounge set, her feet encased in satin mules, not a hair out of place on her blunt-cut bob.

"C'mon in," she said, ushering me into a spacious living room with parquet floors, pristine white furniture, and floor-to-ceiling windows offering panoramic views of the city. French doors led to a terrace as big as my apartment.

It hardly seemed likely Avery had been marrying Chip for his money. If her condo was any indication, it looked like she had scads of her own. Was it possible she actually loved the guy?

"I was just fixing myself a cup of tea," she said. "Can I get you some?"

I'm not much of a tea drinker, but I welcomed the chance to do a little snooping.

"Sure thing," I said.

"How do you take it? Lemon? Sugar?"

"Just sugar is fine."

As she floated off into what I was sure would be a granite and stainless steel wonderland, my eyes wandered to a grand piano covered with framed photos.

I scooted over to check them out.

There were a few photos of Avery dressed to kill on the arm of two older, prosperous-looking gents. I assumed these must have been her former husbands.

But most of the photos were of a young Asian couple, the woman sweet and slightly chubby, the man much taller, with a wide grin and kind eyes. In one photo, they were holding hands; in another, he had his arm slung around her shoulder, hugging her tight.

At first I wondered if they were Avery's children (I still had no idea how old she was), but then I took a closer look and realized that the sweet, slightly chubby woman in the photos was Avery herself.

As I held up one of the photos of the young couple, I heard:

"That's me with my first husband, Sammy."

I turned to see Avery putting a tea tray down on her coffee table.

Then she joined me at the piano, taking the photo from my hand.

"Sammy Suzuki was the love of my life," she said, staring at the picture longingly, as if wishing to go back in time, to be once again leaning into her husband's loving embrace.

"What happened to him?" I asked.

"Died in a freak accident. He was only twenty-seven years old."

With a sigh, she put the photo back down on the piano.

"Here's my second husband, Eliot," she said, pointing to one of the gray-haired gents. "And my third, Jerome."

Somehow, I got the feeling they were interchangeable in her mind.

Abandoning the photos, she perched on one of two sofas flanking a stone fireplace, then motioned for me to sit across from her on the other.

"Here's your tea," she said, pointing to a delicate floral china mug. "I brought some cookies, too."

She held out a plate of dainty sugar cookies.

"Maybe just one," I said, trying to pass myself off as the kind of woman who ate simple, unadorned, chocolate-free cookies.

"After Sammy died," she said, a faraway look in her eyes, "I was utterly shattered. Something inside me died, too. I vowed to never let myself love anyone as intensely as I'd loved Sammy.

"Neither of us had any money," she went on, lost in her memories. "Sammy was a construction worker, and I was a teacher's aide. So after his death, I decided to make something of my life and become an attorney. I was working my way through college as a cocktail waitress at the Peninsula Hotel. You know the Peninsula?"

I nodded.

I'd heard of it, of course—a nosebleed-expensive joint where the Bentley and Bugatti set go to slug down their martinis.

"Anyhow, one night Eliot, my second husband, showed up and fell for me. Before long, he'd asked me to marry him. So I gave up my dreams of law school and became his wife.

"I didn't love him, not the way I loved Sammy. But I admired Eliot and respected him. And as callow as this sounds, I was turned on by his money and power. We were very happy together for four years. Then one day, out on the golf course, he keeled over with a heart attack and left me a very wealthy woman."

She paused to take the world's tiniest nibble of a cookie.

"About a year after Eliot died, I met Jerome. A real estate magnate. Rich and powerful. By then, those were my aphrodisiacs. Six months after our wedding, we discovered he had lung cancer. He was gone within the year."

Another nibble of her cookie. I swear, I'd seen squirrels taking bigger bites.

"Then came Chip. And now he's dead, too."

"I'm so sorry for your loss," I felt obliged to say, trying my best to hide the fact that I'd sorta loathed the guy.

"Chip could be a handful," she said, as if reading my thoughts, "but alone with me, he was surprisingly sweet. I still can't believe he's gone. I know they call me The Widowmaker, and I'm beginning to believe it myself. I should probably come with a warning from the surgeon general."

She put her cookie down without even finishing it.

"Anyhow, I've decided that from now on, there'll be no more men in my life. I can't risk another one dying on me."

Then she blinked as if waking from a dream.

"My God, I've been chattering forever. I've probably bored you to tears."

"Not at all," I assured her.

And, indeed, I found her trail of dead husbands quite fascinating.

"You said on the phone you wanted to talk about Chip's murder. How can I help?"

"Your cabin was next to Chip's, right?"

"Yes, Chip insisted on separate bedrooms. Which was fine with me; the man snored like a foghorn."

"Did you happen to hear anyone in Chip's cabin the day he got killed?"

"It's hard to say. I'd had a lot to drink at the winery, so I was pretty out of it. I was sleeping most of the time. But at one point, I'm fairly certain I woke to hear Cory arguing with his dad. He sounded really angry."

Bingo! The nail in Cory's coffin I'd been looking for.

"Did you hear anyone else that afternoon?"

"No, but it's possible someone else paid Chip a visit. Like I said, I was pretty out of it."

"Do you think Cory might have killed his dad?"

"Actually, I don't. I doubt he'd have the nerve. I'm guessing Bree was the one who held that pillow over Chip's head. The woman would snuff out her own grandmother for a pair of Jimmy Choos."

"Anybody else who might have done it?" I asked.

"Maybe Denny. He was furious with Chip for firing him." She untucked her legs from where they'd been curled up on the sofa.

"That's really all I know," she said, surreptitiously checking her watch.

My cue to leave.

"I guess I should be going," I said.

"Can I get you some more cookies? I can pack some for you to take home."

I looked down at the plate of cookies, now in my lap, and saw they were all gone.

Oh, Lord. How embarrassing. I'd polished off the whole plate.

But in my defense, they were awfully small, practically microscopic.

Turning down Avery's offer of cookies-to-go, I thanked her for her time and bid her adieu. It wasn't until I was driving home that I thought of all those pictures on her piano.

How odd. Not one of them was of Chip.

Chapter Seventeen

B ack in my apartment, I checked my phone and found a text from Mario.

My oven's on the fritz. Will need to cook at your place. I'll be there at six. Please text me your address.

Damn. I'd forgotten all about my date with Mario. And I certainly didn't want him at my apartment. My cleaning lady (aka me) had been most unreliable lately, and my place was a mess. The very last thing I wanted to do was vacuum.

Won't have time to cook boeuf bourguignon. I'll bring steaks instead.

Steaks? Did someone say steaks?

My fingers flew as I texted him my address. What's a little cleanup when there are steaks on the menu?

Hauling my vacuum cleaner from the hall closet, I wiped off months of accumulated dust and started cleaning.

Thanks to Prozac, my apartment was one big fur-fest.

It took seemingly forever, but at last I'd sucked up every clump of fur, dust bunny, and bagel crumb from my floor. Wiping sweat from my brow, I put the vacuum back in my closet, where it would no doubt hibernate for a disgraceful amount of time.

Next, I started in on my bathroom. No way could I let

Mario see my bras drying on the towel rack or my museum of hair care products cluttering my vanity.

Soon I was on my knees scrubbing out my tub and toilet, my Comet and biceps getting quite a workout.

By the time I finished, I was a sweaty mess. Just as I was about to tear off my clothes and leap into the shower, there was a knock on my door.

It was Mario—twenty minutes early.

He was standing on my doorstep, the slick hipster I remembered from the train—his glossy hair pulled back into a ponytail, arms filled with grocery bags, a tote slung over his shoulder.

I was more than a tad surprised to see he was wearing a white chef's jacket.

He certainly took his cooking seriously.

"Hey, Mario!" I said. "How nice to see you twenty minutes earlier than you said you were going to show up."

Okay, I left out that last part, but I was thinking it, wishing I'd had time to take that shower.

"C'mon in," I said, ushering him inside.

Prozac, who'd slept through the entire racket of me vacuuming, now sprang to life as Mario entered the room. Men have that effect on her.

Racing to his side, she eyed him appraisingly.

He's okay, but I like Sean better.

My sentiments exactly.

Then, sniffing, she realized he'd brought food.

Like a shot, she was rubbing herself against his ankles.

Mi casa, su casa, big boy.

"You remember my cat, Prozac," I said. "She was on the train."

"Yes, I remember. The cat who got steak for dinner." He shook his head, disapproving. "She really shouldn't be eating human food. It's not good for her."

Instantly Pro stopped rubbing herself against his ankles and shot him a filthy look.

Who died and made you a veterinarian?

"Let me help you," I said, taking one of the grocery bags and leading him into my kitchen, Prozac trotting behind us, still sniffing for food.

"Change of menu plan," Mario said, setting grocery bags down on my kitchen counter. "Instead of steak, I decided to make monkfish."

Fish?! I vacuumed my apartment for *fish*?

"We're still having mashed potatoes, though, right?"

"Nah, changed my mind. We're having chopped veggies."

Fish and chopped veggies! Talk about your bait and switch. It was all I could do not to shove him out the front door.

"Where are your pots and pans?" he asked, opening a cupboard only to find it full of pretzels, potato chips, and Oreos.

"You actually eat this stuff?" he asked, wrinkling his nose in disdain.

"Not really," I lied shamelessly. "It's just there in case of a nuclear meltdown. My pots and pans are in my oven."

"You keep your pots and pans in your oven?" he asked, horrified.

"I don't use them very much."

I'll say. They'd been virtually untouched ever since my mom sent them to me many moons ago from the Home Shopping Channel.

"Do you realize," he asked, as he began taking my Shopping Channel pots and pans from my oven, "that you've got a pair of jeans in here?"

He held them out, appalled. "And an umbrella."

"I wondered where these had gone to. I thought for sure I'd lost them. I'll just go put them back where they belong."

I trotted off to stow them in my hall closet on top of my hibernating vacuum cleaner.

When I returned to the kitchen, Mario had finished unloading the groceries.

"Anything I can do to help?" I asked.

Words I'd live to mightily regret.

"Absolutely. You can be my sous-chef."

That said as if he were King Arthur, magnanimously offering me a seat at the Round Table.

"You can start by peeling the carrots and onions."

I spent the next fifteen hellish minutes peeling carrots and onions. And, as a bonus chore, cleaning leeks. I don't know if you've ever cleaned a leek, but those things have more dirt than a potting shed.

Between vacuuming, scrubbing the bathroom, and cleaning leeks, I was beginning to feel like a scullery maid.

"Now it's time to chop the veggies," Mario said, once again as if granting me a rare privilege.

He whipped out a cutting board from his tote, as well as a set of knives rolled up in a carrying case.

Yikes. The guy had enough knives in there to perform an autopsy.

"Here you go," he said, handing me one of them. "Be careful. It's super sharp."

Gingerly I started cutting the carrots, praying I wouldn't lose a finger.

Meanwhile, Mario was unwrapping a most unappetizing blob of white fish. Prozac, at his feet, started yowling.

Gimme some of that fish! Can't you see I'm starving? It's been a whole thirty-seven minutes since I finished my Minced Mackerel Guts!

"Be quiet!" Mario said, glaring down at her. "No meowing in the kitchen!"

Prozac hissed, furious.

What nerve! Nobody talks to me that way! If you think I'm ever going to let you give me a belly rub, you are sadly mistaken!

I was still busy chopping veggies when Mario caught sight of my handiwork.

"For crying out loud, Jaine," he said, oozing exasperation. "Have you never watched a TV cooking show? Those slices are way too big."

Grabbing the knife from my hand, he said, "I'll cut the veggies. Just take your cat, and I'll call you when dinner's ready."

Thrilled to make my escape from Mario, whom I'd now dubbed Kitchen Hitler, I gathered Pro in my arms and hustled off to the bedroom, where I plopped down, spread-eagled, on my bed.

Pro sat beside me, tail thumping.

Can you believe it? He actually told me to stop meowing. He's probably the only man on the planet who doesn't think I'm adorable.

I spent the next few minutes soothing her nerves with a relaxing back scratch.

Before long, Prozac was out like a light, and I, too, had sunk into a deep post-vacuuming, veggie-chopping slumber.

I was awakened sometime later by a knock on my bedroom door.

"Dinner's ready," Mario called from the hallway.

I sat up, groggily, then suddenly came to with a start. Never, and I mean never, had my apartment smelled so good. Whatever Mario had done with that fish, it smelled divine.

Eagerly I hopped out of bed and trotted off to my dining room, Prozac hot on my heels.

Not only did the apartment smell great, but Mario had magically transformed my Straight Outta Ikea dining room into a romantic dinner venue, with dimmed lights, candles on the table, and soft jazz playing in the background.

"May I?" he said, holding out a dining chair for me.

My, oh, my. This was nice.

Kitchen Hitler had suddenly morphed into Mr. Manners.

And it was then that the magic really began.

Mario brought out our dinner from the kitchen: sautéed monkfish on a bed of chopped veggies, swimming in butter sauce.

Never had I dreamed fish could taste this good.

True, there were no mashed potatoes, but Mario had picked up a crusty French baguette to sop up the butter sauce.

All served with a most delightful chardonnay.

The meal was so yummy, I didn't even mind when Mario chided me for slipping slivers of fish to Prozac.

As I scarfed down my chow, Mario told me about the restaurant he wanted to open one day, rambling on about the menu, the wine list, the locally sourced produce, the indoor pizza oven, and the outdoor lounge.

Or maybe it was an outdoor pizza oven and indoor lounge.

To be perfectly honest, I was too busy inhaling my monkfish to pay much attention, nodding on autopilot and throwing in an occasional "How nice."

I finally snapped out of my reverie when he asked, "Can I get you seconds?"

Indeed he could—and he did.

A huge smile spread across his face as he watched me dig into Part II of monkfish and veggies. Apparently, the guy really did like to watch me eat.

"Time for dessert," he said when I'd cleaned my plate. "I didn't have time to make profiteroles."

Fingers crossed dessert wasn't going to be something sensible like sorbet or—gasp!—fresh fruit.

"Instead I made Swedish chocolate cake."

Yay! Two of my favorite words. Chocolate and cake.

"It takes only twenty minutes to make, and it's fantastic."

The man did not lie.

Fantastic didn't do the cake justice—gooey chocolate on the inside, with a crisp chocolate crust and topped with gobs of whipped cream.

I was in chocolate heaven.

But I came crashing back down to earth when Mario took my hand and said, "Why don't we make ourselves comfortable on your sofa?"

Oh, crud. I only hoped he didn't want to start playing kissy-face. The guy was a fantastic cook, but I just wasn't into him. And besides, I hadn't quite forgotten Kitchen Hitler.

Warily, I joined him on the sofa, putting as much space between us as possible.

"C'mere," he said, patting the sofa cushion next to him. "I want to show you something."

I forced myself to inch closer, prepared to push him away if he tried any funny stuff. But much to my relief and surprise, he took out his phone and opened YouTube.

"Check out this great video I made on knife-chopping skills."

Knife-chopping skills?

I spent the next thirteen minutes and fifty-four seconds (I was counting) watching a demo of Mario chopping carrots, onions, and rutabaga, and trying desperately not to yawn.

I was beginning to think I would have rather had him kiss me.

"Very interesting," I managed to say when it was finally over.

"I know," he agreed. "I'm an excellent teacher, and the camera loves me."

Then he gazed into my eyes with an intensity that made me more than a tad nervous.

"I guess it's about that time," he said.

Uh-oh. Any second now, he was going to zero in for a smooch.

But, no. That didn't happen.

Instead he said, "Time for me to pack up my knives and the leftovers."

Wait, what? He was taking the leftovers?

I'd been counting on digging into the Swedish chocolate cake the minute he walked out the door.

Soon he came out from the kitchen, his tote filled with leftover fish, wine, and chocolate cake.

"It's been fun," he said.

"Yes, fun," I agreed, barely restraining myself from reaching into his tote and snatching that chocolate cake.

Then he pecked me on the cheek with a chaste kiss and hurried off into the night. Oh, well, I thought, leaning back against my front door. I may not have gotten to keep the leftovers, but I couldn't deny dinner had been dee-lish.

In fact, I was feeling quite happy about the way things had turned out until I walked into the kitchen and turned on the light.

Holy mackerel.

It looked like a tornado had just blown through.

Mario had left every pot, pan, bowl, and dish out on the counter for me to clean. Not to mention all the glop he'd spilled on my stovetop.

It took me what seemed like centuries to mop up the mess.

When I was finally done, I stomped off to my bedroom, adding Kitchen Hitler to my impressively long list of Worst Dates Ever.

You've Got Mail!

To: Jausten
From: Shoptillyoudrop
Subject: The Talk of Tampa Vistas

Daddy is getting on my every last nerve perfecting his Elvis "persona" for the costume party. Not only has he ordered an Elvis costume and wig, he bought a body mic so he can blast everyone's eardrums at the party singing "You Ain't Nothing But a Hound Dog." Which, by the way, he's been practicing all day, every day—out of tune.

As if his singing weren't bad enough, he keeps trying to swivel his pelvis like Elvis. I've warned him he's going to throw out his hip, but does he listen to me? Of course not!

Needless to say, I make him turn off the body mic when he rehearses inside, but every time he leaves the house, he turns it on and announces, "Elvis's cousin has left the building!" The neighbors are complaining. Poor Mildred Kimble says he's been waking her from her naps.

And you should see him at the clubhouse, handing out his autograph as "Elvis's cousin" to everyone he runs into, whether they want it or not, and talking in a ridiculous southern drawl, calling the men "bubba" and the women "ma'am" or "little lady."

Worst of all, he calls me his "hunka hunka burning love." The other day, he did it in front of Reverend Steinmuller! I thought I'd die.

I swear, he's the talk of Tampa Vistas.

Oh, dear. He's started rehearsing again. Must buy some earplugs.

In the meanwhile, it's time for fudge therapy.

XOXO,
Mom

To: Jausten
From: DaddyO
Subject: The Talk of Tampa Vistas

Well, little lady, I'm proud to report that your very own Daddy is the talk of Tampa Vistas. Everyone has been so dang impressed that I'm Elvis's cousin. They've even been asking me for my autograph!

Meanwhile, back home, I've been busy perfecting my rendition of "You Ain't Nothing But a Hound Dog." I've studied Elvis singing it on YouTube, and I've pretty much got his accent down to a T. Not to mention that pelvis action of his. I swear, Lambchop, my hips are swiveling faster than a salad spinner. I can't wait till my wig and costume show up!

Love 'n munches,
Daddy

To: Jausten
From: Shoptillyoudrop
Subject: A Rat's Nest with Sideburns

Lord help me. Daddy's Elvis and Lady Elvis costumes just showed up, along with his Elvis wig, and they're worse than I could have possibly imagined.

The costumes are gaudy eyesores. Bell-bottom jumpsuits studded with blinding, neon-colored "jewels." If Daddy expects me to wear that Lady Elvis monstrosity to the costume party, he's sadly mistaken.

And the wig! My God, it's like a rat's nest with sideburns! Even worse, it stinks to high heaven.

XOXO,
Mom

To: Jausten
From: DaddyO
Subject: Vegas in our Living Room

Fabulous news, Lambchop!

The Elvis costumes just showed up, and they're knockouts— Las Vegas come to life in our living room! I can't believe your mom is refusing to wear hers. (As they say in Graceland, she's done gone plumb crazy.)

And you should see my Elvis wig! I just tried it on, and if I squint in the mirror, I swear I'm looking at Elvis himself.

It has a slight chemical smell, which I'm sure will go away in no time.

Don't pay any attention to your mom if she tells you it stinks to high heaven. Confidentially, I think she might be just a wee bit jealous of all the attention I've been getting lately.

Love 'n snuggles from
Daddy

To: Jausten
From: Shoptillyoudrop
Subject: Good News at Last!

At last, a piece of good news! Lydia Pinkus just called to invite me and Daddy to a lecture she's giving at the clubhouse about Betsy Ross. Lydia's such a dynamic speaker, and her chats are always so educational! I can't wait to hear what she has to say about her illustrious ancestor!

XOXO
Mom

P.S. As you already know, Daddy hates Lydia's lectures—he says they should be cleared by the FDA as a cure for insomnia—so I'm hoping he'll refuse to go.

The last thing I want is to appear in public with Elvis's cousin.

XOXO,
Mom

To: Jausten
From: DaddyO
Subject: Unmasking the Truth!

Guess what, Lambchop? The Battle-Axe has invited us to
one of her snoozefest lectures. This one on—who else?—
Betsy Ross. Normally, I avoid her lectures like the plague,
but not this time. It just so happens your resourceful Daddy
has done a bit of online research and has discovered that
the story of Betsy Ross sewing the first American flag is
just a myth! I can't wait till the Q&A portion of the lecture
to reveal the truth about La Pinkus and her grubby little
ancestor.

Later, alligator!
Daddy

To: Jausten
From: Shoptillyoudrop
Subject: Darn it all!

Darn it all. Daddy says he's coming to Lydia's lecture.

XOXO,
Mom

P.S. Just discovered I'm all out of fudge. Must run to the mall
for a new box.

Chapter Eighteen

I woke up the next morning cringing at the memory of my disastrous date with Kitchen Hitler. But on the plus side, at least my apartment was sparkle clean.

With Prozac howling to be fed, I pried myself out of bed and tootled off to the kitchen.

"Can you believe the nerve of that guy?" I asked Pro, scrubbing a few bits of dried-up glop from my stovetop I'd missed last night. "Hogging the leftovers and leaving me with all that mess to clean up?"

Pro, who'd been hovering at my ankles, thumped an impatient tail.

Yeah, right. What a bummer. Blah blah blah. Now where's my breakfast?

Ever the obedient cat servant, I sloshed a can of Hearty Halibut Innards in her bowl, then nuked myself a cup of coffee and cinnamon raisin bagel, slathered as usual with butter and strawberry jam.

After polishing off my breakfast, along with *The New York Times* crossword puzzle, I checked my emails and read the latest updates on Daddy's Elvis-mania and Mom's life as a budding fudge-o-holic.

Poor Mom. If only there were some way she could inject the stuff intravenously.

But I couldn't worry about my parents, not when I still had a pesky murder to solve.

My thoughts drifted back to my meeting with Avery. How strange that there was no picture of Chip on her piano. After all, she was about to marry the guy. What's more, she was remarkably dry-eyed in the wake of his murder. If she was feeling any grief over Chip's death, she sure hid it well.

The only one she seemed to be grieving was her first husband, Sammy, the construction worker who died in a freak accident.

Hoping to learn more about him, I googled Avery. But all that popped up were pictures of Avery at galas with Chip and her tycoon husbands. No photos or even a mention of Sammy. Clearly he'd been deemed un-newsworthy by the media.

I racked my brain trying to think of his last name. If I remembered correctly, it was the same name as a motorcycle. Yamaha? Nah, that wasn't it. It was Suzuki! Sammy Suzuki.

So I googled Sammy Suzuki, construction worker, accidental death.

But all I got for my efforts were a bunch of obits for Sam, Samuel, and Sammy Suzuki, none of whom was a construction worker, and all of whom were in their seventies and eighties.

Then it occurred to me. What if Sammy was an American version of a Japanese name?

So, once again turning to wizards at Google, I found a list of Japanese boys' names. First I tried Isamu, then Osamu.
Nada.

The third try, however, was the charm.

I typed in Masami Suzuki, construction worker, accidental death. And this time, I hit pay dirt.

From the *Fresno Bee*'s archives, I found the following:

Man Plummets to his Death at Muscle Factory Construction Site

Masami Suzuki, 27, plunged to his death when the scaffolding he was standing on gave way at the construction site of a new Muscle Factory gym. Suzuki's family has filed a wrongful death lawsuit against Muscle Factory, Inc., citing unsafe working conditions.

Muscle Factory executives were unavailable for comment.

That was it. The link I was looking for. Chip Miller, however indirectly, had been responsible for the death of Avery's beloved first husband.

A compelling motive for murder, wouldn't you say?

I had to go to the supermarket to pick up some Dobie Pads and 409 cleaner, both of which I'd run out of mopping up Mario's mess. Avery's place wasn't far from the market, so after picking up my cleaning supplies (and some Double Stuf Oreos, if you must know), I stopped by Avery's condo, hoping she'd be home.

Indeed she was, opening the front door with a smile on her face and a glass of champagne in her hand.

Peering behind her, I could see a bunch of people out on her terrace, seated at a dining table, laughing and chatting, the champagne flowing.

At the sight of me, Avery's smile vanished.

"What are *you* doing back here? I thought I'd gotten rid of you."

Okay, so what she really said was, "Hello, Jaine," but I could sense she was more than a tad irritated to find me on her doorstep.

"I'm afraid you've come at a bad time. I'm hosting a family brunch."

She started to close the door, but with lightning speed, I whipped out the article I'd printed from the *Fresno Bee* and shoved it in her hand.

She took one look at it and sighed.

"Okay," she said wearily, "you can come in, but just for a few minutes. I'll be right back," she called out to her family on the terrace. "Enjoy the quiche!"

I followed as she led me to her luxe bedroom, a bright, airy space with room enough for two armchairs and a chaise longue.

A framed photo of her beloved Sammy sat on a night table next to her bed.

She sank down into one of the armchairs and motioned me to sit in the other.

"Okay, so now you know. Chip was responsible for Sammy's death. We tried suing him, but thanks to his team of piranha lawyers, he got off scot-free."

She shook her head in disgust.

"From that day on, I vowed to get revenge. I had nothing back then, no money, no power. So I changed my name from Aiko to Avery, dropped twenty pounds, and married my way into money, all the while intending to make Chip pay for what he'd done to Sammy.

"I kept track of him over the years, but he was always either married or in a relationship. Then, at last, the time was right. My third husband had died, and Chip's umpteenth girlfriend had given him the heave-ho.

"So I managed to 'accidentally' cross paths with him at

a charity gala. Lucky for me, he had a thing for Asian women. We started dating, and before long, he proposed. Finally, the coast was clear. Time to move in for the kill."

"So you sneaked into his cabin and smothered him with a WORLD'S BEST DAD throw pillow!" I cried triumphantly, quite pleased with myself for having uncovered the killer.

"Of course not!" Avery replied, indignant. "I wasn't going to kill Chip. I was going to marry him and—with the help of my own team of piranha lawyers—take him for every penny he was worth in a messy divorce.

"But things worked out even better than I'd hoped. Chip was murdered!" she beamed, taking a celebratory sip of her champagne. "Gone for good! What a relief never again to have to look at that preening egomaniac, let alone go to bed with him. Unlike his Iron Man persona," Avery confided with a wry smile, "Chip's libido was in the basement. On the few times he could rise to the occasion, it was over faster than a flu shot.

"But it was still hell being with him, and I'll be forever grateful to whoever killed him. Here's to Chip's killer," she said, raising her champagne glass in a toast. "May you get away with it and live a long and happy life."

With that, she polished off the rest of her champagne.

"Anything else I can do for you," she asked, "before I return to my family?"

A slice of quiche would be nice were the words I was wise enough to keep to myself.

"No, I appreciate your taking the time to talk with me," I said instead.

Then I followed Avery as she led me out to the front door.

"If you think of any more questions," she said with a brittle smile, "don't come bothering me. I've said all I'm going to say."

"Right-o," I replied, as she all but shoved me out the door.

I made my way to the elevator, the laughter from Avery's terrace echoing in my ears.

Maybe Avery had been telling the truth. Maybe all she wanted was to bleed Chip dry in a messy divorce. Then again, maybe the thought of actually being married to Chip was so abhorrent, she'd worked up the courage to knock him off.

And so I drove home that day with my cleaning supplies, Double Stuf Oreos, and—most important—a hot new murder suspect.

Chapter Nineteen

A very may have catapulted herself to the top of my suspect list, but Cory and Bree were still very much in the running.

Avery claimed she heard Cory arguing with Chip in his cabin the afternoon of the murder. And I'd seen the happy couple celebrating in their pool, Bree telling Cory how proud she was of him, and how everything worked out just as they'd planned.

The next day I drove over to their house unannounced, once again hoping to catch them off guard. This time, I came armed with a quart of macaroni salad I'd picked up as a condolence offering, extra cash for bribing my way past the cleaning lady—and dressed in old sweats, just in case I had to do battle with their filthy hedges.

As it turned out, I did not have to bribe my way past the cleaning lady or do any hedge-battling, because Cory himself answered the door, opening it just a crack as he peered out at me.

"Can I help you?" he said, stone-faced, not exactly rolling out the welcome mat.

"Hello, Cory. Remember me? Jaine Austen? I was working with your dad on his book. Anyhow, I stopped by to pay a condolence call and to tell you how sorry I am for your loss."

"I'm afraid Bree and I are too overcome with grief to see visitors."

Grief, my fanny! I thought, as I heard salsa music blaring from somewhere in the house. I wouldn't have been surprised to find a conga line out on their pool deck.

"I brought macaroni salad," I said, hoping to entice him with an offering of food.

"Thanks."

He reached out to snatch it from my hand, and as he did, I saw he was dressed in tennis whites.

Meanwhile, I heard Bree calling out, "Cory, I can't find my tennis racket!"

"Thanks for stopping by," Cory said. And without further ado, he slammed the door in my face.

If he thought he was getting rid of me that easily, he was sadly mistaken.

I drove off in my Corolla and parked it at the end of the street, where I settled down to wait. Sure enough, minutes later I saw Cory and Bree leave their house with tennis rackets and get into a shiny black Mercedes.

I only hoped Cory hadn't seen my car earlier and wouldn't recognize it as I started following them. But he and Bree seemed blissfully unaware of my ancient white Corolla on their tail.

I followed them to the Hilldale Country Club, a sprawling affair not far from their home in Rancho Park. I'd heard of Hilldale, of course—an exclusive joint known for its lively mix of aging bluebloods and barracuda strivers.

The Mercedes pulled into a parking area out front, but when I tried to follow, I was stopped by a guard at a booth.

"I need to see your membership card, ma'am," he said, giving my Corolla the stink eye.

"I'm not a member," I said, shooting him my friendliest smile. "Not yet, anyway. I'm here to join up."

"Then you'll need to go to the clubhouse. I'll let them know you're coming."

He told me to park my Corolla at the far end of the lot, no doubt to keep it from contaminating the luxury cars parked in front, then pointed me in the direction of the clubhouse, an imposing Spanish hacienda-style building with arched windows and red tile roof.

Waiting for me in the lobby was a bubbly brunette in a Hilldale blazer whose name tag read MARYANNE.

Her bubbly smile lost some of its effervescence as I approached.

"You here about the housekeeper's job?" she asked.

I suddenly remembered I was wearing my grungy, hedge-battling sweats.

"No, I'm here to inquire about membership. Excuse the way I'm dressed; I just came from my women's club annual trash pickup day, beautifying our freeway one exit at a time."

"Is that so?" she said, dubious. "Are you sure you can afford our membership? It starts at fifty thousand dollars a year."

Fifty thou???

It took all my acting skills to keep the astonishment from showing on my face.

"Gee, that is rather pricey, but I know it's what Grammy Buffet would have wanted when she left me all that money. 'If you're going to do something,' Grammy Buffet used to say, 'do it first class.'"

"Grammy Buffet?" Maryanne blinked in surprise. "Any relation to Warren Buffet, the billionaire tycoon?"

"Confidentially, yes, but please don't tell anyone. Uncle Warren is a stickler for privacy."

Now her smile was back, bubblier than ever.

"You can depend on my discretion," she gushed, my new BFF. "Let me show you around the clubhouse."

All I really wanted to see were the tennis courts, but I faked enthusiasm as she led me on a tour of the clubhouse, proudly showing off their formal dining room, casual Grill Room, card room, and several private meeting rooms.

Never had I seen a more impressive collection of plaid golf pants and Botoxed foreheads.

I made cooing noises about how lovely everything looked, secretly counting the seconds till we got outside. All the while, Maryanne was yakking up a storm about Hilldale's world-class chefs, carefully curated wine list, dinner dances, and celebrity golf tournaments.

After being shown a third empty meeting room, I managed to pipe up, "It's all so lovely, but I'm especially interested in seeing your tennis facilities."

"Of course!" Maryanne cooed. "But first you've got to see our magnificent golf course and our Olympic-sized swimming pool."

At long last, she led me outside.

"There's the golf course," she said, pointing toward what looked like acres of grassy green velvet.

"Very impressive," I said.

"Brad Pitt shot a hole in one here during one of our celebrity tournaments."

Babbling about how Brad was even more handsome in person than he was on the silver screen, she led me down a path to the aforementioned Olympic-sized pool, where bronzed one percenters were either lounging on chaises or doing arduous laps in the pool.

"The children's pool is over there," she said, pointing to

a kiddie pool in the distance, "so if you're a lap swimmer, you won't be disturbed."

"Good to know," I said, secure in the knowledge that I'd need a ferry to make it from one end of the ginormous pool to the other.

Finally, when I was on the verge of clamping my hand over her mouth to shut her up, Maryanne uttered the words I'd been longing to hear.

"And now, let's check out the tennis courts."

I followed her down another path to the club's seven tennis courts, relieved to see Cory and Bree on one of them, volleying with gusto, Bree shrieking with glee every time she scored.

If those two were in mourning, I was Serena Williams.

I needed to confront them with what I'd discovered, but I couldn't possibly get near them, not with Maryanne glued to my side.

Time for Operation Dump Maryanne.

"This is all so fantastic," I said. "Just what Grammy Buffet would have wanted for me. Luckily I brought my checkbook. I'd like to become a member right now."

"Of course!" Maryanne was beaming like she'd just won the lottery. Clearly the woman was working on commission. "Just come with me to my office."

I followed her back into the clubhouse, but before she could trap me in her office, I said, "I need to use the ladies' room, if I may."

"No problem! For 50K a year, you can use the men's room, if you want."

Okay, she didn't really say that, but I sure was thinking it.

"Right this way," she said, leading me down one of the clubhouse's many corridors till we reached the ladies' room. "My office is down the hall, last room on the right. I'll be waiting for you with papers to sign."

And off she trotted, eager to ring up a sale.

I slipped inside the ladies' room, where I waited a few minutes to give Maryanne a chance to get to her office, then poked my head out the door. The corridor was empty.

Needless to say, I did not head down the hall to Maryanne's office. Instead, I scooted off in the opposite direction, working my way through a labyrinth of hallways until at last I saw an exit door.

I pushed it open, hoping it wouldn't set off an alarm, and breathed a sigh of relief when it didn't. Then I stepped out into an alley lined with trash cans, a space for employees only, hidden from the members by a cedar fence laced with morning glories.

At the end of the alley, I came to a gate. Opening it, I was thrilled to see the tennis courts not far from where I was standing, Cory and Bree still whacking away at a tennis ball.

I was there in a flash.

"Hey, guys!" I said, bounding onto their court.

"What're *you* doing here?" Bree asked, irritation blazing from what I suspected were tinted blue contact lenses.

"I could ask you the same question. I thought you two were too overcome with grief to see visitors. But apparently not grief-stricken enough to miss a tennis game."

Cory had the good grace to look abashed.

But not Bree.

"It just so happens," she said, "that physical exercise helps process grief, because it releases endolphins."

"I think you mean endorphins."

"I'm pretty sure it's endolphins."

And I was pretty sure she had the IQ of a turnip.

"I don't care what you call them," Bree pouted. "We're still grief-stricken."

"Oh, really? Well, it also just so happens that Avery heard Cory arguing with his dad in Chip's cabin the day of the murder. What's more, I just so happened to see you guys at your pool the other day, celebrating with umbrella drinks and talking about how everything worked out just like you hoped it would."

"You sneaked onto our property?" Bree sputtered. "We should have you arrested for trespassing."

"I wouldn't call the police if I were you. The last thing you need is the cops looking into your lives right now."

"Listen, Jaine," Cory said, eager to placate me. "It's true that I was in my dad's cabin the day of the murder, but I only was there to tell him I was sick of being his whipping boy. We argued, but I didn't kill him. When I left my dad's cabin, I swear he was still alive."

"I can vouch for that," Bree said. "I was there, too."

Oh, please. As if I could believe anything that came out of Bree's mouth. She'd swear they were both hiking the Himalayas that afternoon if she thought she could get away with it.

"What about the stuff I overheard at the pool, how everything worked out just like you planned?"

"It's true everything worked out like we'd planned," Cory said. "I'd just convinced the Muscle Factory's board of directors to let me take over as CEO of the company. That's why we were celebrating."

I didn't doubt that Cory had wangled himself the CEO gig. But that still didn't let him off the hook for murder. He seemed especially uneasy, staring down at the ground, unable to make eye contact.

But Bree had no such trouble.

"Get out of here right now," she said, glaring at me, "or I'm calling Security."

With that, she swung her racket and slammed her bright green tennis ball right at me, missing my skull by millimeters.

"Oops!" she said with a venomous smile. "Did my ball almost hit you on the head and give you a concussion? Sorry about that! Accidents happen. So be careful, Jaine."

I know a threat when I hear one, and I'd just heard one.

Call me crazy, but I was beginning to think the killer half of that duo might very well be Bree.

I hurried off to the clubhouse and was sprinting across the lobby when I bumped smack-dab into Maryanne.

"Where've you been?" she cried. "I've been looking all over for you!"

"Sorry, Maryanne. I've got to run. Just got a call from Uncle Warren. Turns out Grammy Buffet might not be dead after all."

Okay, so I don't lie well under pressure.

"Your grandmother might not be dead after all?" she blinked.

"Yes, a miracle recovery."

"In that case, be sure and give her my card. I'd love to sign her up as a member at Hilldale."

Yep, she worked on commission all right.

I bolted off to my Corolla, feeling bad about the whoppers I'd told Maryanne, and more convinced than ever that Bree might be the killer.

You've Got Mail!

To: Jausten
From: Shoptillyoudrop
Subject: Off to the Lecture!

We're off to Lydia's lecture on Betsy Ross. In honor of the occasion, and to carry on the tradition of her illustrious ancestor, Lydia's sewn her own suit. If I didn't know better, I'd swear it was an original Coco Chanel. Lydia's always been a wonderful seamstress, and now I know why. It's in her blood!

Instead of moping and sulking like he usually does when faced with a Lydia lecture, Daddy actually seems eager to go. In fact, I've never seen him so enthusiastic about attending one of Lydia's events.

Maybe at last he's realized how dynamic Lydia can be once she gets behind a podium.

XOXO,
Mom

To: Jausten
From: DaddyO
Subject: All Systems Go!

Your mom and I are headed off to the Battle-Axe's lecture on Betsy Ross—where I intend to reveal the truth about Lydia's phony-baloney ancestor and how she never actually made America's first flag.

Can't wait to see the look on the Battle-Axe's face when I expose her as the pompous poseur she really is.

Love 'n snuggles from
Daddy

To: Jausten
From: Shoptillyoudrop
Subject: Utter Humiliation!

What a fool I was to think Daddy would behave himself at Lydia's lecture!

Things got off to a rocky start the minute we left the house and Daddy announced, with his body mic on, that Elvis's cousin had left the building. He had the darn thing taped to his chest. Needless to say, I made him turn it off. He swore he only wore it to announce his departure from the house. (He actually thinks the neighbors *like* his megawatt news bulletins!)

At first everything at the lecture went wonderfully well. Lydia did a PowerPoint presentation, showing us portraits of her famous ancestor—along with a photo of the pattern she used to make her Chanel suit.

Lydia told us that, according to historians, Betsy Ross did not actually sew America's first flag, that it was made by a man named Francis Hopkinson. But even though she didn't sew the original stars and stripes, Betsy ran a thriving business making flags for the U.S. Navy—a rare feat for a woman of her day.

Not only that, she was married three times, had seven children, and lived to the ripe old age of eighty-four!

So caught up was I in Lydia's fascinating tale, I didn't notice that Daddy had fallen asleep. I can't say I was surprised, as he usually winds up nodding off at Lydia's lectures. But then, much to my horror, he started snoring. Somehow as he slumped down in his seat he must have activated his body mic, because soon his snores were reverberating throughout the auditorium. I cringed as everyone stared at us, then quickly jabbed Daddy awake and made him turn off his dratted mic.

I thought the worst was over, but was I ever wrong.

Lydia wrapped up her lecture to an enthusiastic round of applause and asked if there were any questions or comments.

Right away Daddy leapt up from his seat, turned on his body mic, and began ranting about how the story of Betsy Ross sewing the first American flag was just a myth and that the person who actually made the first flag was Francis Hopkinson.

He had no idea Lydia had already said as much in her lecture, because he'd been sound asleep. Everyone looked at him like he was nuts. But that didn't stop him.

"Betsy Ross was a fraud!" he cried. "Unlike my cousin Elvis Aaron Presley, a national treasure who brought joy and blue suede shoes to countless Americans!

"While I'm at it, may I say, Lydia, that your fines on overdue library books, ban on exotic pets, and No-Gnomes lawn policy are a travesty of justice!"

By now everyone in the audience was gaping at him, appalled, and soon two Tampa Vista security guards had shown up to escort him out of the auditorium.

The last thing we heard after they hauled him away was, "Elvis's cousin has left the building!"

Talk about humiliating. I'm so mad, I could spit.
XOXO,
Mom

P.S. His ghastly Elvis wig is still stinking up the house! I'm *thisclose* to dumping it in the trash.

To: Jausten
From: DaddyO
Subject: A Triumph!

I'm proud to tell you, Lambchop, that my speech at the clubhouse was a triumph.

True, I dozed off and missed the part of Lydia's lecture where she admitted Betsy Ross didn't actually sew the first American flag. But I used my bully pulpit to get in a few shots about Lydia's despotic rule as president of the homeowners association.

And even though I was escorted from the auditorium by two Tampa Vistas security guards (no doubt sicced on me by one of Lydia's toadies), I could tell everyone was moved by my stirring speech.

Love 'n kisses from
your triumphant,
Daddy

P.S. I'm very disappointed in your mom. She's actually annoyed at my heroic effort to stand up for truth, justice, and blue suede shoes!

Chapter Twenty

Why is it that Lance always shows up just as I'm about to eat breakfast?

The next day, I'd settled down on my sofa with my coffee and cinnamon raisin bagel and was reading about Daddy's cameo performance at Lydia's lecture when Lance came banging at my front door.

"Emergency!" he cried, rushing into my apartment and grabbing half of my bagel.

"Tonight's the night of the Empire Club cocktail party, and I've been so swamped at work, I haven't even begun to do your makeover."

He looked at me in my coffee-stained chenille bathrobe and shook his head in dismay.

"I've got less than a day to magically transform you from bagel-swilling couch potato to Romanian royalty!"

"I see you're not too noble to do some bagel-swilling of your own," I pointed out, eyeing my bagel clutched in his hand.

"But don't worry," he said, oblivious to my snark, "I'm up to the challenge! As soon as I get back from the gym, I'm taking you to a party dress rental shop. And then off to my friend Lars for hair and makeup."

"I still don't understand how you're going to pass me

off as Romanian royalty. I don't speak a word of Romanian, and I doubt I'll be able to fake a Romanian accent. What if somebody there speaks Romanian and asks me a question?"

"Not to worry. We'll say you have laryngitis, and I'll do all the talking."

So what else was new? He does that all the time anyway.

"All you have to remember is that you're Contessa Anastasia Magdalena, third cousin once removed of the late King Michael, and you live in a charming villa outside the tiny town of Rasnov."

"Is this a real place, or did you see it on an episode of *The Munsters*?"

"It's a real place, Jaine. I've done my research. Everything about you is going to be absolutely authentic. Except for you, of course.

"Now I'm off to the gym. Be ready when I get back! We've got a full day ahead of us."

Sure enough, as threatened, about two hours later, Lance showed up at my apartment and carted me off to a joint called Elegant Party Rentals in the heart of Hollywood.

Living up to its name, the place was pretty darn elegant, with plush peach carpeting, racks of meticulously displayed gowns lined up against the walls, cubbyholes for dress shoes, and a mannequin dolled up in head-to-toe sequins.

We were greeted by a steely reed of a gal who looked like she could actually be Romanian royalty—her jet black hair swept back in a severe bun, milky white skin stained with blood-red lips.

"Hi, there," Lance said. "I need a gown that will make my friend look like a European countess."

She looked me over and practically rolled her eyes.

"Sorry, sir. I just rent party dresses. You want miracles? Go to Lourdes."

Okay, so what she really said was, "I'd be delighted to help."

Lance was no longer paying attention to her, however, riffling through the gowns on the rack.

"Omigod, this is it! It's so Audrey!"

He held out a floor-length black dress, cinched in at the bodice, then flaring out from the waist. And indeed it looked exactly like something the waiflike Audrey Hepburn, with her impossible 22-inch waist, would have worn.

"Are you kidding, Lance? I'm never going to squash myself into that."

"Don't be silly. All you need is some extra-strength shapewear."

"Absolutely not. No shapewear! The last time I got trapped in a tummy tucker, I had to cut myself out with a pair of cuticle scissors. Never again."

"How about this?" the saleslady asked, holding out a preposterous slinky gown with cut-outs strategically placed to reveal every inch of my love handles.

"Let me look," I said, scanning the racks until I found the perfect outfit: a two-piece, floor-length number: navy chiffon skirt with—be still my heart!—an elastic waistband, and a flowy beaded top.

"Oh, my God." Lance moaned, "You'll look like the mother of the bride in that thing."

"It's actually quite popular," the saleslady chimed in. "We just got it back from a woman who wore it to her ninetieth birthday party."

"You've got to take the Audrey dress!" Lance insisted.

Nuh-uh. No way on earth was I going to put myself through shapewear hell.

"Sorry, Lance," I said, playing hardball. "No elastic waist, no Contessa."

For one of the few times in my life, I held the bargaining chips, and Lance could see I wasn't going to back down.

"Oh, well," he sighed, conceding defeat. "Romania isn't exactly known as the fashion capital of the world. We'll probably get away with it. But at least let's get you a pair of stylish shoes. What about these?"

He pulled out a pair of gorgeous black satin pumps with a high stiletto heel.

"They're beautiful!" I cried.

And indeed they were. Off I scooted to the dressing room to try on my Romanian royalty outfit. The elastic waist was très comfy, giving me plenty of room to chow down on hors d'oeuvres. And the shoes, while just the teensiest bit tight, were so swellegant, I couldn't pass them up.

"So what do you think?" I asked, coming out from the dressing room and spinning around for inspection.

"It just might work," Lance said, eyeing me appraisingly. "The more I think about it, the dowdy look is perfect for Romanian royalty. Very Old World conservative. I can pass you off as an eccentric aristo!"

"That dress is so *you*!" beamed the saleslady.

I suspected that wasn't exactly a compliment, but who cared? It had an elastic waist, and I was a happy camper.

For the time being, anyway.

Lance paid a whopping two hundred bucks for the rentals—"It's worth it to get into the Empire Club"—and off we headed to see his buddy Lars, a studio hair and makeup guy, who, luckily for us, was between movie assignments.

Lars lived in a charming 1920s fourplex in West Hollywood.

A tall guy with a beaming smile, Lars came to the door in linen shorts and a Hawaiian shirt, his white-blond hair gelled into stiff spikes.

"Good to see you, buddy!" he said to Lance, then turned to me.

"You must be Jaine, the Chunky Monkey addict."

"Guilty as charged," I said, wishing Lance wouldn't go around sharing my food preferences with the world at large.

"Come on in, and let's get started," Lars said.

We followed him to his island-themed living room, furnished with rattan patio furniture, palm-frond wallpaper, and a mini tiki bar.

The only thing that clashed with the island paradise theme was a salon stylist's chair in the rear corner of the room.

"I use it for my private clients," he explained.

"I need Jaine to look like a Romanian countess," Lance said. "So go ahead and work your magic."

"A countess, huh?" Lars said, his smile fading ever so slightly. He then led me into his kitchen, where he washed and conditioned my hair with some heavenly coconut-scented products.

"First thing we need to do," he said when he had me seated in his stylist's chair, "is get rid of these nasty split ends."

Soon he was snipping away, and when he liked what he'd done, he took out his dryer and blew my hair into a sleek, shiny bob.

"I love it!" I cried.

"I'm not so sure," Lance said, frowning. "It's a little too Runway Model at Fashion Week. She doesn't have the cheekbones to pull it off."

Of all the nerve! I happen to think I have perfectly serviceable cheekbones. But no one was asking my opinion, so it was back to the kitchen to wet down my hair again.

Poor Lars wound up cycling through three more styles—natural curls, 1950s French chignon, and beachy waves.

None of which met with Lance's approval.

By now, Lar's welcoming smile had long since bit the dust.

"I know!" Lance cried, no doubt still yearning for the Audrey dress we'd seen at Elegant Rentals. "How about Audrey Hepburn in *Breakfast at Tiffany's?*"

And so, after yet another trek to the kitchen sink, Lars was blowing out my curls and sculpting my newly straightened hair into an elegant updo.

And before I could stop him, his scissors were back in action, giving me Audrey bangs. Which was the last thing I wanted. I'd just spent the last six months growing them out!

I looked down in dismay at my shorn hair lying in clumps at my feet.

"Perfect!" Lance cried, when Lars was done.

True, the bangs looked quite cute now that Lars had straightened them to within an inch of their lives, but I dreaded to think of the mini-Brillo pads they'd turn into the minute they got wet.

"She's so Audrey in *Breakfast at Tiffany's*!" Lance beamed.

Maybe from the neck up, but from the neck down, I was Ma Kettle at an all-you-can-eat buffet. I just hoped my Elegant Party Rentals chiffon dress would amp up my image.

Another half hour slogged by while Lars slathered my face with makeup. And then, at long last, I was released from the stylist's chair.

It was hard to tell which one of us was more relieved to see me go, but I figured it was probably Lars.

"I owe you," Lance said to Lars, who looked like he'd just been through the Punic Wars and back.

"Big time," Lars agreed, rubbing a crick in his neck, his formerly spiky hair, like Lars himself, now limp and lifeless.

"You guys let yourself out. I'm just going to get myself something to drink."

The last thing I saw as I headed out the door was Lars at his tiki bar, pouring himself a tall glass of vodka.

Chapter Twenty-one

L ance dropped me off at my apartment with strict instructions.

"I'll be back at six o'clock. No eating whatsoever. And don't move a hair on your head."

Was he kidding? After four solid hours with Lance playing Henry Higgins, I was in dire need of a fistful of Oreos and a nice relaxing soak in the tub.

The minute he left, I inhaled the Oreos, then trotted off to run a bath.

I dug out a jumbo shower cap from my bathroom cupboard, but saw that it was way too small to cover my *Breakfast at Tiffany's* do.

I couldn't risk having my hair curl in the steam from the tub, so I came up with the genius idea (if I do say so myself) of wrapping my sleek new do in Saran Wrap. Soon my Audrey hair had been sealed tighter than a mummy in King Tut's tomb.

Prozac looked up from where she'd been napping on the sofa, staring at my head.

Anything to eat in there?

Armed with just the weensiest glass of chardonnay, I trotted back to the bathroom to soak my stress away.

"What a day!" I moaned to Pro, who had followed me and was now sprawled out on the toilet tank. "I'm exhausted."

Tell me about it. I just had to walk all the way from the living room to the bathroom.

"I only hope they serve decent chow at the cocktail party."

At the mention of food, her little ears perked up.

Don't forget to bring back leftovers.

"Do you think I have a snowball's chance in hell of passing myself off as a Romanian countess? I really hate to let Lance down, after all the money he's laid out."

She gazed at me lazily.

I didn't hear anything about me in all that, so I'm going to go ahead with my nap.

And just like that, she was conked out, snoring like a buzzsaw.

I lay back in the tub, thinking about my upcoming performance at the Empire Club, hoping that (a) I would do Lance justice, and (b) they'd be serving franks in a blanket.

After a heavenly half hour of fantasizing about nibbling on hors d'oeuvres and Hugh Jackman, I dredged myself out of the tub to get dressed.

Unfortunately, when I unwrapped my head, I was dismayed to see that the Saran Wrap wasn't quite as effective as I'd hoped.

My bangs had curled up in the humid tub air. I shoved open the window to air out the bathroom, then raced to my bedroom where I spent the next fifteen minutes trying to straighten my bangs.

At last I got them reasonably straight. Not quite as straight as Lars, but with any luck, Lance wouldn't notice the difference.

After spraying them to cardboard consistency, I got

dressed in my two-piece gown, once again grateful for the elastic waist. I checked myself out in the mirror and breathed a sigh of relief. I could barely notice the slight curl in my bangs and thought I looked quite elegant in my flowy evening ensemble.

It was when I tried to slip on my shoes that panic once again set in.

Apparently my long soak in a hot tub had caused my feet to swell.

The gorgeous satin stilettos that had pinched just a wee bit this morning were now awfully tight. How on earth would I get through the next few hours encased on these four-inch foot vises?

I raced to the kitchen and tried icing my feet with a bag of frozen Tater Tots, which helped a little.

When I slipped on the shoes again, they were still too tight, but I was pretty sure I could make it through the next few hours.

I didn't have time to fret about my feet, because just then Lance showed up in a miasma of spicy aftershave, dressed to the hilt in a designer suit, his blond curls sculpted to perfection.

His smile froze at the sight of me.

"My God, what happened to your bangs?"

"Nothing! Nothing at all!" I lied shamelessly.

"You didn't do something stupid like take a shower, did you?"

"Absolutely not," I assured him. And technically, that wasn't a lie.

"Oh, well. There's nothing to be done about it. Just remember to look haughty. And stand up straight. You're Romanian royalty, not Igor at the Frankenstein's."

Yeah, well, it's hard to have perfect posture when you're trying to balance on four-inch stilettos.

"Hey, I just had a great idea! Instead of stilettos, why don't I wear flip-flops?"

"Flip-flops?" Lance, cried, wide-eyed with disbelief. "Are you insane?"

"Didn't you say you were going to pass me off as an eccentric aristo? Nothing says eccentric more than flip-flops at a cocktail party."

"Forget it, Jaine," he said, grabbing me by the wrist. "Let's get out of here."

As he pulled me out the door, I heard Prozac meowing from the bathroom.

Don't forget those leftovers.

Chapter Twenty-two

For the second time in two days, I was headed off to a ritzy social club.

But the Empire Club, as I was about to discover, was worlds apart from Hilldale. Housed in a former boutique hotel in West Hollywood, its members were light-years younger and hipper than the Hilldale gang.

On the drive over, Lance had yakked about how club members enjoyed not one but two private dining rooms, a ballroom, a bowling alley, a 24-hour gym, and a rooftop pool.

"I've just got to get in!" he said before handing over his Mini Cooper to a valet.

"Remember," Lance whispered to me as we walked into the hotel lobby, "if anyone asks you anything, just point to your throat and shake your head. That's when I'll leap in and do the talking."

Milling inside the lobby were a bevy of hot young things dressed to kill. And those were just the guys. All of them cooler than cool, some sporting scruffy face stubble, others wearing high-tops.

Heck, I could've worn my flip-flops after all.

The gals were pretty darn spectacular, too, many of them

wearing the kind of slinky, cut-out dress the saleslady had shown me at Elegant Party Rentals.

Feeling a tad out of place in my mother of the bride outfit, I prayed Lance and I would be able to pull off this Romanian royalty stunt.

We took an elevator up to the club's ballroom, a dazzling venue replete with crystal chandeliers and ornate crown molding. The hardwood floors had been buffed to a gleaming shine. Normally I love hardwood floors, but now, with my feet encased in my increasingly tight stilettos, I groaned at the sight of them. What I wouldn't have given for some plush wall-to-wall carpeting.

But I was soon distracted by the heartwarming sight of cater waiters dashing around with trays of wine and hors d'oeuvres.

Before I could hail down a waiter, we were greeted by Lance's boss at Neiman's, Kelvin, a tall African American guy with piercing eyes and granite cheekbones.

"Good to see you, Lance," he said. "This is Contessa Anastasia Magdalena, I presume?"

"Indeed it is," Lance beamed.

"So glad you could join us," Kelvin said, giving me the once-over with those piercing eyes. "Love your dress. My grandmother has one just like it."

Word of my arrival spread, and before long, we were surrounded by a group of club members eager to meet European royalty.

Lance told them about my laryngitis.

"She gets it from screaming at the servants, ha ha."

Lance continued to spin his tale about how I was the third cousin once removed of the late King Michael and how I lived in my villa outside the tiny town of Rasnov.

"The villagers simply adore her," Lance blathered.

"Every year, she awards first prize at Rasnov's cabbage roll cook-off."

I wasn't paying much attention to his chatter, still distracted by the steady flow of waiters passing out hors d'oeuvres. I was in chowhound heaven, eagerly digging into a parade of tasty tidbits.

Behind me I could hear someone whisper, "She may not be able to talk, but she sure can eat."

The only fly in this culinary ointment were my feet, which were killing me.

Standing on those damn stilettos, I felt my toes practically welded together in my shoes. Just when I was thinking I was going to need my feet surgically removed from my shoes, I heard someone call out, "Hi, Jaine!"

I looked up and saw a waiter approaching.

Omigosh. It was Sean! And he was coming right at me with a tray of filo-dough pastry.

Lance's eyes wide with alarm, he sprang into action.

"I'm afraid you're mistaken. This woman is Contessa Anastasia Magdalena of Romania."

I shot Sean a pleading look, praying he wouldn't blow my cover.

"So sorry, your highness," Sean said. "I thought you were someone I know, but now that I see you up close, I realize I'm mistaken."

I was so shaken by my near exposure, I could barely swallow the pastry I'd snatched from Sean's tray.

Sean wandered off, and Lance continued the saga of Contessa Anastasia Magdalena: How I loved to ride my horse, Vladimir, at sunrise and sip wine from my private winery at sunset.

As he yammered on, I saw Sean heading down a hallway, probably off to the kitchen to restock his tray. Eager to talk with him and explain what was going on, I barked out a hoarse "'Scuze. Be back momentito" in my best Natasha Badenov accent.

Then, as fast as my aching tootsies allowed, I scurried across the room and down the hallway where Sean had disappeared.

I spotted him headed toward the kitchen.

"Sean!" I called out, hobbling after him. "Wait up."

He turned and saw me.

"Jaine! What the heck was going on out there?"

"It's a long story, but the bottom line is I'm pretending to be a Romanian countess to help out my neighbor. He's desperate to join the Empire Club, and he's trying to impress them by claiming to be best buds with European royalty."

"You're kidding. What an insane thing to do!"

"That's Lance. Insane pretty much covers it. You won't say anything to anyone, will you?"

"Don't worry," he laughed. "Your secret is safe with me."

He should've been hurrying off to the kitchen, but he lingered there, gazing at me.

"So what's going on in your life when you're not pretending to be a Romanian countess?"

"Same old same old. Still trying to find Chip's killer."

"Having any luck?"

"Not much. What about you?"

"I'm working on an investigative journalism story and took a part-time waiting gig at Mimi's Bistro in Santa Monica. You should stop by and say hello."

He zapped me with a smile that sent my heart doing somersaults.

But then I remembered how he'd dashed out of Paco's Tacos to meet up with his "hon" of a girlfriend/wife/fiancée.

Which meant I was chopped liver.

"Well, gotta get back to work," he said. "Rich people need their hors d'oeuvres."

And off he went to the kitchen. I stared after him longingly, then headed back to resume my role as Contessa Anastasia Magdalena.

I was hobbling down the hallway when I came upon a blessed sight: the ladies' room.

I dashed inside and collapsed onto a velvet settee, prying my aching tootsies free from the stilettos. It felt like they'd just done five to ten in a state penitentiary.

Thank heavens the lounge was empty so I could massage them in peace.

I spent the next several minutes working on my feet, trying to get the blood flowing back in their veins. But I couldn't stay there forever. Lance was probably wondering where I was.

Reluctantly, I tried to squeeze my feet back into the stilettos, but it was mission impossible. Try as I might, I simply couldn't jam them in. Desperate, I hid the shoes behind a faux ficus and hurried out to the hallway, bumping into a svelte young thing on her way in.

" 'Scuze," I said, once again channeling Natasha Badenov, and dashed back to join the others, hoping no one would notice my bare feet.

"Welcome back, Anastasia, darling," Lance said, daggers in his eyes. "I was just telling the others how we met when you were at Neiman's trying on shoes."

Damn, why was he talking about shoes? Someone was bound to notice my bare feet. But, miraculously, no one did.

Just when I thought I was getting away with it, I felt someone tapping me on the shoulder.

It was the svelte young thing I'd bumped into in the hallway.

"Excuse me, Contessa," she said, holding up my abandoned stilettos, "but I think you left these in the ladies' room."

Now everyone was staring at my toes peeking out from under my mother of the bride skirt.

Hell. It was all over now.

But Lance wasn't about to give up.

"Omigod," he chuckled, "that's *so* Contessa Anastasia Magdalena! She goes barefoot all the time. In fact, she often rides her horse, Vladimir, bareback *and* barefoot. Back in Rasnov, they call her the Barefoot Contessa."

Man, he sure knew how to sling the bull poo.

And surprisingly, the others seemed to buy it. At least I hoped they did.

But Lance had had enough of our little charade.

"I'm afraid we've got to get going. The contessa just flew in from Romania this morning. Jet lag and all that."

"Glad you could stop by," Kelvin said to Lance, shaking his hand. "And lovely to have met you, Contessa," he added, turning to me, skewering me with another piercing glance.

Was it my imagination, or did I hear quote marks around the word "Contessa"?

Lance led me out of the ballroom, holding my elbow in a death grip.

Once we were outside, he exploded. "I can't believe you were walking around barefoot!"

"My feet were killing me, and when I took off my shoes to massage my feet, I couldn't jam them back in. I told you I should've worn flip-flops."

"And what about that bit with the waiter?" Lance wanted to know. "The one who called you Jaine?"

"He's a guy I met on that train trip to Santa Barbara."

"Well, I can kiss the Empire Club goodbye. Kelvin wasn't buying any of it. Did you see the way he was looking you?"

By now we were at the valet stand, waiting for Lance's Mini Cooper.

"I'm so sorry, Lance," I said, taking his hand in mine. "I really wanted this to work."

And just like that, he deflated.

"It's okay. You tried your best. And besides, I don't want to hang out with these people anyway.

"They're such a bunch of phonies," he whispered before turning to the valet and informing him, "My other car's a Maserati."

Chapter Twenty-three

I was on my sofa the next day, icing my feet, trying to recover from stiletto-gate, when the phone rang.

In a burst of crazed optimism, I answered it, hoping it was Sean.

Maybe he'd been so captivated by the sight of me in my Audrey Hepburn updo, he'd dumped his "hon" and was calling to pledge his undying love.

But of course it wasn't Sean.

It was Chef Mario.

"You free for dinner tomorrow night?" he asked.

No way. Absolutely not. Not after the FEMA-grade disaster he'd left behind in my kitchen.

"I'm making that boeuf bourguignon I promised you," he said. "Along with scalloped potatoes and chocolate cream pie for dessert."

Chocolate cream pie? Be still, my heart.

But no. I had to remain strong.

"See you at seven?" he asked.

"Sounds great!"

Omigod, I've got to face facts. My name is Jaine, and I'm a food-a-holic.

I definitely needed to check into a twelve-step program.

(I just had to find one that served Danish along with their coffee.)

In the meanwhile, I needed to concentrate on more important stuff, like tracking down Chip's killer.

Remembering Bree's tennis ball whizzing past my cranium, I decided to pay a visit to Cory's sister, Cassidy. I'd ruled her out as a suspect since she wasn't even on the train at the time of the murder, having gone back to L.A. with her motorcycle buddy. But I wanted to chat with her to see if she thought Cory—or, more likely, Bree—was capable of killing Chip.

After consulting Versel's contact list, I gave her a call.

"Who is this?" she asked, sounding frazzled as she answered her phone.

"It's Jaine Austen. We met on your dad's train. I was hoping you'd have time to talk with me about your father's murder."

"I can't right now. I'm in a bit of a jam. I'm supposed to be showing my paintings in Beverly Hills today, and my car just broke down. Would you be able to give me a lift?"

"Glad to," I said, grateful for the opportunity to talk to her.

She gave me her address, and I headed over to her apartment in Venice. I remembered her telling me that she was an artist, and I was impressed that she was showing her work in a Beverly Hills gallery.

I was far less impressed, however, when I saw where Cassidy lived—a sun-faded stucco apartment building adorned with security bars on the windows and a jungle of graffiti on the walls.

Cassidy was standing on the curb near a battered black Volvo, looking very Surfer Gypsy in a flowing gauze skirt and peasant blouse, her Botticelli curls caught up in a chiffon headband.

She waved at me eagerly after I'd parked my Corolla and headed to her side.

"Thanks so much for coming to my rescue, Jaine."

The trunk of her Volvo was open, and I gulped at the sight of the canvases stacked up inside.

I'm no art connoisseur, but in my humble op, Cassidy's paintings were, to put it as kindly as possible, stink-o-rama. Not much better than the stuff you see pinned up in kindergarten classrooms.

"How interesting," I managed to say.

"I paint with my heart," Cassidy said, gazing at her work.

Next time try using a paint brush was the advice I kept to myself.

But, hey. For all I knew, her paintings were considered fine art by connoisseurs. After all, I reminded myself, she was showing at a Beverly Hills gallery.

I helped her load the paintings into my Corolla, along with a couple of easels, somewhat puzzled when she also tossed in two lawn chairs.

Maybe the chairs were part of her exhibit, some kind of art installation.

As we climbed into my Corolla, Cassidy gave me the address of the gallery, and I entered it in to my GPS system.

And off we went, Cassidy yakking about her art and how fulfilling it was to release her creativity to the universe. She was in the middle of a discourse about the healing powers of color when I heard the GPS lady announce, "Your destination is five hundred feet ahead on your right."

By now, we were on the fringes of Beverly Hills, not an art gallery in sight.

All I could see five hundred feet ahead was a gas station.

This couldn't be right.

"I'm sorry," I said. "I must have entered the wrong address."

"Nope," she replied. "We're at the right place. I come here every week to sell my paintings. The gas station doesn't mind. Yusef, the owner, lets me park my car and use the ladies' room. He's very sweet."

Yikes! She was selling her stuff at a gas station! Her art *was* stink-o-rama.

I helped her unload her paintings—landscapes, portraits, still lifes—one more amateurish than the next. She took three of the least offensive paintings and displayed them on easels. The rest she stacked up against the pole with the gas prices.

"Here," she said, handing me a lawn chair. "Pull up a chair so we can chat."

I sat across from her on a plastic woven lawn chair, saggy from years of weary tushes.

"So what did you want to ask me about Chip's murder?"

"First, let me offer you my sincerest condolences."

"Thanks, but we weren't very close. Chip wasn't my biological father, you know."

She'd certainly lucked out of that gene pool.

"He was actually a pretty pathetic guy. Underneath his bluster, he was very insecure, always trying to convince the world—and, more importantly, himself—how great he was. He tried to build himself up by dragging everybody else down."

When I first saw Cassidy on the Iron Man Express, meditating with her crystal, I'd written her off as a hippy-dippy airhead. But now she seemed a lot more insightful than I'd given her credit for.

"Growing up," she continued, "I saw how toxic he was and tried to stay out of his orbit. He made my adoptive mom's life pretty miserable, belittling her and cheating on her right and left. She was a kind woman and didn't deserve to be treated so badly. When she died, the official cause was heart failure, but I think she'd just lost the will to live.

"He's awful with Aunt Versel, too, but she's stronger than my mom. She can take it."

I had to agree. Versel seemed feisty enough to take on the Spanish Armada.

"Chip was always begging me to come work with him at The Muscle Factory, offering me a huge salary. But I watched him emasculate Cory and I didn't want him destroying me, too.

"Unlike Cory, I've never cared about money. Mom left me a small nest egg in her will, and I pretty much live off that. Plus the money I make from my art sales," she added.

Which, given the total lack of interest from people walking past the gas station, I figured was bupkis.

"Anyhow, Chip could be pretty awful, but he didn't deserve to die."

I wasn't sure I agreed with her on that one, but I managed to murmur some comforting sounds, then plowed ahead.

"This is really awkward, but do you think there's any chance your brother might have done it? After all, he seemed to be very angry with Chip that day at the winery."

"Oh, Cory loathed Chip, that's for sure. But he'd never have the nerve to actually kill him."

"What about Bree?"

"Bree? She's a whole other story. I wouldn't put anything past her. The woman radiates bad karma. I can easily picture her smothering Chip with a throw pillow."

My sentiments exactly.

"Anyone else you think might have done it?"

"Maybe Denny," she shrugged. "Now that Cory is CEO of The Muscle Factory, he's kept Denny on, and in fact, from what I hear, Denny's the one who's really in charge. Cory wants the money and prestige from the title, but he doesn't want to do the work.

"All in all, things have worked out pretty well for Denny. With Chip alive, Denny would have been out of a job. But now, he's running the show. So if you're looking for suspects, you should check him out."

Which is exactly what I intended to do.

All the while we'd been talking, people had walked by Cassidy's display, still ignoring her paintings. One or two had stopped to look, but quickly hurried off.

"Sales have been down lately," Cassidy said, watching a couple walk away after taking a peek at her stuff. "I think it must have something to do with the stock market."

Yeah, right. Of course. That explained it.

"But like I said, I'm not in it for the money. I've already got everything that matters to me: The sun, the sky, the fresh air!"

That said as we breathed in exhaust fumes from the cars pulling up to the gas pumps.

I was feeling really sorry for her when one of the passersby—a pink-haired gal in shorts and bare midriff, her navel ring glinting in the sun—took a look at one of the paintings and stopped in her tracks.

"Omigosh! I love it," she cried. "This is exactly what I've been looking for!"

Thank goodness, a sale!

"How much are you asking for it?"

"Ten dollars."

"I'll take it."

With that, she handed Cassidy a ten-dollar bill and removed the canvas from the easel. But instead of taking the canvas, she stacked it up along with the others against the gas price pole and grabbed the easel.

"I've been looking for an easel like this everywhere. And they're so darn expensive.

"Thanks so much!" she said, waving goodbye.

I was mortified for Cassidy, but she took it in stride.

"I find most of my easels on the curb on trash day. That was ten bucks sheer profit," she smiled, happily lifting her face to the sun.

By now I was tired of breathing exhaust fumes.

"I really should get going," I said. "Would you like me to come back later to take you home?"

"No, that's okay. I'll get a ride from Michael, the man who came to pick me up at the winery."

I remembered the handsome motorcycle guy who'd spirited her away and figured they were probably an item.

"What an awful day that was," she said with a sigh. "No way was I going to get back on that train."

If only I'd been smart enough to follow her lead, I wouldn't be in the pickle I was now.

"Thanks so much for your time," I said, getting up.

I was about to walk away, but then I took a last look at Cassidy's orphan paintings, leaning against the gas price pole.

I doubted she'd make a single sale that day. Unless she sold another easel. Or a lawn chair.

Feeling a sudden rush of sympathy, I found myself saying. "You know what? I'd like to buy one of your paintings."

"Really?" Her eyes lit up. "That's great. Which one?"

"This one," I said, picking up the painting the gal with the pink hair had rejected.

It was a still life of pears and apples. Or they might have been oranges and kiwis. It was hard to tell.

"It's so . . . vibrant!" I managed to say, handing her ten bucks.

Then I bid her goodbye and hustled home, stopping off en route to get rid of the painting at the nearest thrift shop.

Chapter Twenty-four

"I'm sorry, but we don't take artwork."

I was standing at the door of the UCLA Thrift Shop, holding Cassidy's still life of unidentifiable fruit.

"Are you sure?" I said, pointing to a bunch of paintings on the wall behind her.

"I'm sure," she said, looking down at Cassidy's canvas, "that we're not taking this."

Ouch. It was a good thing Cassidy wasn't there to witness this devastating (yet kinda accurate) appraisal of her work.

I brought the painting home, only to have Prozac take one look at it and yowl in protest.

Take it away! I may go blind!

Fortunately, the next day was garbage pickup day, so I left it out on the curb next to my trash cans, hoping a passerby with poor vision would adopt it.

But the next morning it was still there.

With a pang of guilt, I put it in the trash bin.

After the garbage trucks had come and gone, I went outside to bring in the cans. And you're not going to believe this, but the painting had been tossed out on the lawn.

Rejected by the Department of Sanitation!

I brought it inside and stashed it in the hall closet. Eventually I'd figure out a way to get rid of it, but right then I had more pressing matters to attend to.

Namely, Denny, Chip's former right-hand man, now the guy in charge at The Muscle Factory.

I remembered how furious he'd been when I'd overheard Chip firing him, and his ominous threat: *It's your funeral. I'm going to see to that.*

Wasting no time, I put in a call to Muscle Factory headquarters and was connected with Denny's secretary.

"Who's calling?" she asked.

"Jaine Austen, a writer Denny met on a recent train trip."

"Just a sec," she said, then I heard her call out:

"A writer named Jaine Austen for you. Says you met on a train trip."

"Tell her I'm not in," I heard Denny shout out in reply.

"He's not in," the secretary replied.

"Yes, so I heard."

Time to bring out the big guns.

"Tell him I want to interview him for a cover story in *Los Angeles Magazine.*"

Of course, I was doing no such interview. But I figured it might open the door.

"She wants to interview you for *Los Angeles Magazine,*" the secretary said.

"Tell her to stop by at five o'clock."

Voilà. I was in. All it took was a little bit of imagination and a big fat lie.

Of course, the downside of my big fat lie was the string of big fat anecdotes I had to listen to as Denny prattled on for the pretend interview I was conducting.

"Where's the photographer?" he asked, when I first showed up.

He'd stood from behind his desk to greet me, biceps bulging in a Muscle Factory tee, his buzz cut trimmed with military precision. And I suspected he'd spritzed on some extra spray tan for the event.

"They'll send someone out in a day or two," I vamped. "They always send the writer out first."

Meanwhile, off to the side, a janitor was taking down a framed poster of Chip and replacing it with one of Denny.

"Was this Chip's office?" I asked when the janitor had gone, glancing around the cavernous corner room.

"You betcha!" Denny grinned. Then, realizing he was supposed to be mourning the passing of his boss, and conveniently forgetting his barely suppressed glee when I'd first told him that Chip was dead, he added a not very convincing, "Sure gonna miss that guy."

I sat down across from him as he launched into an endless monologue about The Muscle Factory, how it was the greatest gym ever and how he intended to make it even better.

I nodded through it all, pretending to take notes (but actually writing my grocery list), wondering how I was ever going to segue from Denny the Great to Chip's murder.

"C'mon," he said, after he'd finished a blow-by-blow description of his years playing college football. "Let me take you on a tour of the place."

And so he began toting me around to the workout rooms, the racquetball courts, the swimming pool—where impossibly fit people were burning more calories in an hour than I did in a year.

As we walked along the hallway, I saw the same janitor from Denny's office taking down a poster of Chip and replacing it with one of Denny.

Clearly a new king had been crowned at The Muscle Factory.

Denny was showing me a room full of people working out on treadmills when he spotted someone he knew.

"Talk about coincidence!" he said. "Look who's here. Teresa Madden."

"Teresa Madden?" I asked.

"Your managing editor at *Los Angeles Magazine*. She works out here all the time."

Before my horrified eyes, he bounded over to a sleek brunette with no discernible body fat, racing on her treadmill at Indy 500 speed.

"Hey, Teresa!" Denny beamed. "Thanks for the cover story!"

"What cover story?" Teresa asked, not breaking her stride.

"The one *Los Angeles Magazine* is doing on The Muscle Factory."

She finally came to a halt and blinked, puzzled.

"I don't know what you're talking about. We're not running a story on The Muscle Factory."

"But here's the writer you sent to interview me," he said, pointing at me. "Jaine Austen."

Teresa looked at me like the perfect stranger I was.

"Unless she's the one who wrote *Pride and Prejudice*, I have no idea who this woman is."

Denny whirled on me, livid.

I cringed at the thought of the poop that was about to hit my fan.

"Gotta go," he said to Teresa, grabbing my arm in a steely grip.

"Explain yourself!" he sputtered as he shoved me out into the hallway.

"I'm sorry I fibbed about *L.A. Magazine*, but it was the only way I could get in to see you. The police think I may have killed Chip, and I'm trying to clear my name. Can you give me just a few minutes of your time? It's vitally important."

I plastered on a look of utter desperation, which was easy to do since I was pretty darn desperate.

"Okay," he sighed, taking pity on me. "But make it fast."

I couldn't possibly let him know I suspected him of killing Chip.

So instead I asked him if he had any idea who the killer might be.

"Haven't a clue. Everybody hated Chip. It could have been any of the others. All I know is it wasn't me. I won't pretend I'm sad he's gone. He was about to screw me over, just like he screwed over his first business partner, Scotty Dickens. Scotty built the gym from the ground up, only to get kicked to the curb by Chip."

I remember Versel mentioning Chip's first business partner and how he'd done all the heavy lifting to get The Muscle Factory up and running.

"And what an ego!" Denny was saying. "Those WORLD'S BEST DAD pillows. The WORLD'S BEST LOVER plaque over his bed. And his face plastered all over the gym."

I tactfully refrained from pointing out that it was now Denny's face plastered all over the gym.

"Do you mind my asking," I said, girding my loins and hoping he wouldn't go ballistic, "where you were at the time of the murder?"

"Yes, I mind. Very much. But if you must know, I was in my cabin on the phone with my attorney, talking to him about suing Chip for wrongful termination."

Our chat was interrupted just then by the arrival of a refrigerator of a security guard, who promptly proceeded to frog-march me out to the parking lot.

Soon I was driving home, my upper arm throbbing from where Denny's security goon had been clutching it. In spite of my ignominious exit from the premises, I couldn't help thinking that when Denny insisted he hadn't killed Chip, he'd sounded pretty believable.

That is, until I remembered what he said about the WORLD'S GREATEST LOVER plaque in Chip's cabin. I'd seen the plaque when I discovered Chip's body. At the time, I was too distracted by Chip's corpse to pay much attention to it. But it was there, all right.

And now I wondered how Denny could have known about it, unless he'd been in Chip's cabin, smothering the life out of his tyrannical boss.

Chapter Twenty-five

Of course, it was always possible Denny had seen Chip's WORLD'S BEST LOVER plaque before the afternoon of the murder. But there'd been a definite Do Not Cross line between Chip and his underlings, and I doubted Chip had ever invited Denny to chew the fat with him in his inner sanctum.

Meanwhile, back at my apartment, I found a text from Mario, reminding me of our dinner date that night.

Damn. I was supposed to be at his place in West Hollywood at 7 o'clock. And it was already 6:40.

I had no time to do my hair and makeup, but I didn't care. I was so not in the mood to see Mario, remembering his stultifying chatter about the restaurant he someday planned on opening, and the even more stultifying video of him demonstrating his knife skills.

Why on earth had I agreed to a rematch with this guy?

Then I remembered: Boeuf bourguignon! Scalloped potatoes! And chocolate cream pie!

I may not have cared about seeing Mario again, but my taste buds were raring to go, practically screaming at me to get my fanny in gear.

But first I had to feed Prozac, who was rousing herself from her umpteenth nap of the day.

"Here you go, hon," I said, sloshing some Minced Mackerel Guts in her bowl.

She glared at me balefully.

That's right. Go off and chow down on boeuf bourguignon while I'm stuck here eating mackerel guts.

Somehow she can always sense when I'm going out to dinner. And she resents it every time.

Ignoring her stink eye, I was about to dash out the door when I realized I didn't have a host gift for Mario. There was no time to stop off and buy him a bottle of wine. And somehow I didn't think he'd appreciate the bag of Tater Tots in my freezer.

Then I remembered Cassidy's painting. I'd bring that! What a perfect way to unload it.

Unearthing it from the hall closet, I sighed to see that it had not, regrettably, become any less of any eyesore while in storage. Oh, well. Maybe Mario would like it. One man's trash is another's treasure and all that.

Soon I was in my Corolla, heading off to West Hollywood, Cassidy's mystery-fruit painting on the passenger seat beside me.

Parking was tough, and I circled around for what seemed like forever until I finally found a spot about five blocks away from Mario's apartment. By now, it was 7:15, the minutes ticking by as I lugged Cassidy's painting to Mario's place.

I was beginning to regret not bringing Mario those Tater Tots.

Finally, I made it to my destination—the Sweetzer Arms, a 1970s apartment building with a huge VACANCY banner strung across the balconies of several front-facing apartments.

Whatever security system they had was clearly on the fritz, because I breezed my way into a lobby littered with

Chinese takeout menus and took the elevator to Mario's apartment on the fourth floor.

He came to the door in his chef's jacket, an apron tied at his waist, his hair coralled into a ponytail. At the sight of his emerald-green eyes and glossy black hair, I once again thought of how attractive he'd be to lots of gals.

But not, alas, to me.

Besides, I wasn't paying all that much attention to his looks, immediately bowled over by the aroma of something yummy in the oven. My boeuf bourguignon!

"C'mon in, Jaine!" he said, ushering me into his apartment.

"I brought you something to thank you for having me over to dinner."

I handed him Cassidy's painting, waiting for him to take one look at it and cringe.

But much to my surprise, he beamed with delight.

"This is great! Thanks so much. I love it!"

Hurrah! I'd dumped Cassidy's fruitpourri onto a grateful recipient!

Between my joy at unloading the painting and the aroma of boeuf bourguignon, I was feeling very happy indeed that I'd said yes to this date. What a fool I'd been to even think about turning it down. So what if I had to endure a harmless video about knife-chopping skills?

"Guess who just stopped by?" Mario said. "My mom. I invited her to join us for dinner."

Fine by me. I didn't care who was sitting at the table as long as one of the guests was boeuf bourguignon.

My happy bubble was about to burst, however, when I followed Mario into his beige-on-beige living room, where a stout fireplug of a woman with neon orange hair and a most disconcerting unibrow stood, arms crossed over her sofa cushion-sized chest.

"Mom," Mario said, "meet Jaine. Jaine, this is my mom, Nelly."

The fireplug looked me up and down, distinctly unimpressed.

"Lovely to meet you, Nelly," I said.

"Mrs. Fanelli to you," she snapped in reply.

Then she turned to Mario, radiating disapproval.

"*This* is the girlfriend you were telling me about?"

Wait, what? He told his mom I was his *girlfriend*??

"Ptui!" Mrs. F. sniffed. "You can do better than her."

"Mom!" Mario cried, embarrassed. "I'm so sorry," he said, turning to me. "Mom didn't mean it."

"Of course I did!" Mrs. F. insisted. "And what's that?" she added, pointing to Cassidy's painting.

"A gift Jaine brought me."

"To thank Mario for inviting me to dinner," I explained.

Mrs. F. (or, as I was now calling her, Mrs. F.U.) eyed the painting, about as impressed with it as she'd been by me.

"You call this a hostess gift?" she tsked. "You never heard of wine? Cheese? Baked ziti?"

"Mom," Mario was pleading, "be nice."

"I call 'em as I see 'em," she said, unrepentant. "But on the plus side, at least she's got nice, wide childbearing hips." Glaring at me from under her unibrow, she added, "I want lots of grandchildren."

And then, in full-tilt drill sergeant mode, she commanded, "Smile!"

As I did, she grabbed me by my cheeks.

"Good gums," she nodded in approval.

Omigod, I felt like a horse at auction. Any minute now, I expected her to snap on rubber gloves and check out my lady parts.

But what was bothering me most of all was that Mario

thought I was his girlfriend. I didn't care how good a cook he was, I had to end this thing ipso pronto. I made up my mind: As soon as I finished my second slice of chocolate cream pie, I was outta there.

"Time to eat!" F.U. announced, leading the way to a small dining area where a dinette table was set for two with fancy wineglasses and linen napkins, a jar of breadsticks in the middle of the table.

"I'll bring out another place setting for Jaine," F.U. said, heading into the kitchen.

Seconds later she was back with a paper napkin and some dented silverware.

"You two sit down," she said. "I'll serve."

She directed me, of course, to the place setting with the paper napkin and Mario to the seat across from me.

"Mom, I wanted Jaine to sit next to me."

"Change of plan," she snapped, as she waddled back into the kitchen.

"I'm so sorry about this," Mario whispered when she was gone. "She's this way with all my girlfriends."

"Mario, this is only our second time seeing each other. I hardly think I'm your—"

Before I could finish my thought, F.U. had returned with a heaping plate of boeuf bourguignon and scalloped potatoes.

"For you, caro," she said, setting it in front of Mario.

"Mom," Mario chided. "You should serve Jaine first."

"You cooked. You get served first."

Soon she was back with another heaping plate of beef bourguignon and potatoes and—I kid you not—a paper plate with a dollop of beef and even smaller dollop of potatoes.

Needless to say, I got the paper plate.

"Mom! You hardly gave Jaine any food."

"That's okay. She could stand to lose a few pounds."

Look who's talking! I wanted to shout, perilously close to ramming a breadstick up her ying-yang.

"I'll get you some more beef," Mario said to me, about to get up.

"Forget it," F.U. replied. "There's no more left."

"I'm so sorry," Mario said, sitting back down.

For a minute, I thought maybe he was going to give me some of his, but nope.

All he did was hold out the breadsticks and say, "Here. Have another."

I spent the next excruciating half hour or so listening to F.U. yakking about what a precious baby/toddler/teenager Mario had been. And how all the girls loved him.

"Consider yourself lucky," she said to me, as I scraped my plate for bourguignon sauce and slugged down my wine (served, by the way, in a Flintstones jelly glass).

At last we were done with the main course (I'd plowed through mine in nanoseconds). Yes, it had been a truly awful experience, but my taste buds had not given up hope. There was still that chocolate cream pie on the horizon.

I should've known better than to think I was going to get a decent portion. F.U. served me the merest sliver while treating herself and Mario to generous slabs.

"So what about you?" F.U. asked, as I stared down at my sliver of pie. "What do you do?"

"Jaine's a writer!" Mario piped up. "She wrote 'In a Rush to Flush? Call Toiletmasters!'"

Then, turning to me, he added, "I googled you."

Ah. How comforting to know the guy was stalking me online.

"You wrote 'In a Rush to Flush'?" F.U. asked.

For the first time all evening, she lobbed me a smile.

"I love that! It just so happens," she confided, "I'm always in a rush to flush."

Whoa! Way TMI. Especially at the dinner table.

"I think I like her," F.U. said to Mario. "She's a lot better than that roller-derby skank you were dating."

Oh, groan. If there was one thing worse than F.U. hating me, it was F.U. liking me. What if she was pissed off when I stopped seeing her precious Mario and put out a hit on me?

When dinner was finally, mercifully over—me wondering if I was going to wind up in a Witness Protection Program—F.U. got up and started clearing the dishes.

"Mario, you've been on your feet cooking," she said to her beloved son. "Go rest in the living room. I'll be with you in a minute. Jaine can do the dishes."

That's right. For the second time in two dates with this guy, I wound up doing the dishes.

Never again, I vowed to myself, as, huddled in the kitchen, safe from F.U.'s prying eyes, I helped myself to a hefty hunk of chocolate cream pie.

You've Got Mail!

To: Jausten
From: DaddyO
Subject: Hanging Tough!

Dearest Lambchop,

Mom's demanding I apologize to Lydia for my comments at her Betsy Ross lecture. But I refuse to back down in my quest for justice at Tampa Vistas. In a shameless attempt to break my spirit, Mom's enforced her No Meatloaf ban. And guess what? For once, I'm hanging tough. All it takes is willpower, iron resolve, and a Hungry Man Meatloaf Dinner. (Not as good as Mom's, but good enough.)

Everyone's been congratulating me for standing up to the Battle-Axe and decrying her draconian rules! Someone has even started a grass-roots movement to elect me president of the homeowners association!

Love 'n stuff from
Your crusading
Daddy

To: Jausten
From: Shoptillyoudrop
Subject: Delusional

You're not going to believe this, sweetheart, but Daddy refuses to apologize to Lydia for his disgraceful behavior at the Betsy Ross lecture! I've even enforced my No Meatloaf ban, but he won't back down. He's buying frozen meatloaf and mashed potatoes at the supermarket. Which is fine with me. Fewer pots to clean.

And don't listen to Daddy if he tells you everyone in Tampa Vistas is congratulating him for standing up to Lydia. As far as I know, the only person on Daddy's side is Nick Roulakis, who's mad at Lydia for making him take down his lawn gnome.

Daddy's also running around saying someone started a grass-roots movement to get him elected HOA president. The person who started that movement? Daddy! As far as I know, the only two members are Daddy and Nick Roulakis.

Honestly, the man is delusional!

And his silly Elvis wig is still stinking up the house. I'm going to put it outside on the patio right now to air out.

XOXO,
Mom

To: Jausten
From: Shoptillyoudrop
Subject: Oh, Dear!

A squirrel just ran off with Daddy's wig.

To: Jausten
From: DaddyO
Subject: Tragedy!

I was out on the patio taking a break from my "Hound Dog" rehearsal when Mom came outside with my Elvis wig and put it on a patio chair to air it out. She still claims it smells awful, but it's all in her head. I can assure you it doesn't smell any worse than lemon-scented Raid. In fact, I find the scent quite refreshing.

Anyway, I was sitting there, relaxing and thinking of the changes I'll make when I'm president of the homeowners association, when suddenly out of nowhere a squirrel came darting onto the patio and ran off with my prized Elvis wig!

Needless to say, I sprang to my feet and started chasing the critter as he ran down the side of the house and out onto the street. That squirrel was quite a sprinter. I followed as fast as I could—luckily I'm in peak physical shape thanks to my hours of hip-swiveling Elvis rehearsals—but it wasn't easy keeping up with him. At one point I thought I'd lost him when he darted behind a hedge, but he soon emerged and continued zipping down the street.

At last I spotted him on Lydia's front steps, burying my wig in the soil of her potted hibiscus. With lightning speed, I dashed up to her steps and shooed the squirrel away. Then I got down on my knees and dug up the soil in search of my wig, only to find a buried sesame seed bagel!

Darn it all. I must've lost my thieving squirrel when he dashed behind that hedge. And I'd been following the wrong squirrel ever since!

I was looking down at the bagel in dismay when I heard the unmistakable growl of the Battle-Axe.

"Hank Austen, what on earth do you think you're doing?"

Sure enough, I looked up and saw La Pinkus glaring down at me.

"I was looking for my Elvis wig."

"Why would your Elvis wig be in my hibiscus plant?"

"I thought a squirrel buried it here. But I was following the wrong squirrel. The one I finally caught up with was burying this bagel. Would you like it?" I held out the bagel, hoping to placate her. "I'm sure it'll be fine once I dust off the potting soil."

To which she just rolled her eyes and had the nerve to suggest I seek psychiatric counseling.

Then she went inside, got a broom, and made me sweep her front steps.

I swear, the woman is Stalin in support hose.

Love 'n kisses from
Daddy

To: Jausten
From: Shoptillyoudrop
Subject: So Darn Embarrassing

Lydia just called and told me she found Daddy on her front
steps, digging up her hibiscus plant with a filthy sesame seed
bagel.

It's so darn embarrassing. Definitely time to hit the fudge.

XOXO,
Mom

To: Jausten
From: DaddyO
Subject: The Show Must Go On!

Well, Lambchop, you'll be relieved to know I just sent away
for a replacement Elvis wig.

Nothing, but nothing, will stop me in my quest to bring
Cousin Elvis back to life—and win first prize—at the Tampa
Vistas costume party.

Love 'n snuggles from your
Dauntless
Daddy

Chapter Twenty-six

"Worst. Night. Ever."

I groused to Prozac as she sat on my chest, clawing me awake for her breakfast the next morning.

"Mario's mom fed me scraps and then made me do the dishes!"

Prozac gazed down at me, nary a trace of sympathy in her eyes.

That's what you get for not staying home and scratching me behind my ears all night.

"I swear, I've had mammograms that were less painful!"

Pro yawned, still unmoved by my tale of woe.

I spent a most enjoyable evening clawing a hole in one of your sweaters. I won't tell you which one. It's much more fun to let you discover it on your own just as you're getting dressed to go out!

Wearily, I hauled myself out of bed and shuffled off to the kitchen to fix breakfast: Luscious Lamb Innards for Pro and a CRB for moi.

After breakfast, I read about the audacious theft of Daddy's Elvis wig and only hoped the squirrel had the good sense to dump it in the nearest landfill.

Then I texted Mario to thank him for dinner and tell

him that I wouldn't be able to see him again as I'd joined the Peace Corps and was moving to Somalia. That tiny fib, I felt certain, would put an end to any more dinner invites.

Determined to put my ghastly evening with Mario and F.U. behind me, I turned my attention back to my murder suspects.

As far as I could see, the front runners were Bree, Avery, and Denny.

Shuddering at the memory of Bree's tennis ball whizzing perilously close to my cranium, I felt certain she had the nerves of steel to murder Chip. Then there was Avery, who had a whopper of a motive. After all, Chip was responsible for the death of her beloved first husband. And what about Denny? Furious at having been fired by Chip, he could've killed his boss either in a moment of uncontrolled rage—or in a carefully charted plan to retain his gig at The Muscle Factory.

Just when I was convinced one of them was the culprit, another one stepped in and stole the spotlight.

What I needed was a voice of reason, someone to help me untangle my web of suspects. The first person to come to mind was Versel Rush—a no-nonsense, clear thinker if ever I'd met one.

Aside from Sean, she'd been my favorite traveling companion on the Iron Man Express. (Admittedly, the bar was pretty low, but I was a fan nonetheless.)

I called and asked if she was free to meet up for a chat.

"Of course, sweetie. C'mon over, and we can chew the fat."

And so later that morning, I tootled over to Chip's Bel Air estate.

I blinked in amazement when Versel came to the door. Gone were her polyester pants and I BELIEVE IN CHOCOLATE FOR BREAKFAST sweatshirt. Instead, she wore a cashmere lounge set, much like the one Avery had been wearing when I'd first dropped by to visit her at her condo.

Her steel-gray hair, formerly scraped back with a drug-store headband, had been styled to perfection in a blunt-cut, chin-length bob, also a lot like Avery's. It looked like Versel had become a plus-size version of Avery Suzuki Tom-kins Feinberg.

"Wow," I cried, "you look great!"

"I treated myself to a wee bit of a makeover and shop-ping spree," she said with a wink. "Retail therapy really does help in times of stress."

I followed as she ushered me into the living room, done up in manly leather furniture, hunting prints on the wall. The same portrait of Chip I'd seen the janitor taking down at The Muscle Factory hung over the fireplace.

Versel and I sat across from each other on a tufted leather sofa, a coffin-sized coffee table in front of us.

"I figured I could hang around moping about Chip," Versel explained, "or I could start living my life. I haven't got all that many years left, and I decided to make the most of them."

"Good for you, Versel! Chip wasn't worth moping over anyway."

Of course, I didn't add the part about Chip, but we all know it's true, right?

"How'd you like some apple crumb coffee cake," Versel offered, "straight from the oven?"

Indeed, I could smell the enticing aroma of cinnamon and apples wafting from the back of the house.

She didn't have to ask twice.

"Sounds yum!"

She reached over and picked up a silver bell from the coffee table.

"Get this!" she said, tinkling the bell.

Seconds later a diminutive dark-haired maid in a crisp white uniform came scurrying into the room.

"Carmela, hon. Bring us two coffees and some of that apple crumb coffee cake."

"Yes, ma'am," Carmela replied, hurrying off.

"Can you believe it?" Versel whispered as Carmela left. "I have a maid! After all those years waiting on Chip, someone's waiting on me! Sometimes, after Carmela's gone for the day, I ring the bell just for the fun of it."

She grinned in delight.

"I'm thinking of redecorating the living room, too. All this leather reeks of testosterone. I want to do it up in soft gray chenille, with white pine accessories. Like this."

She picked up a *House Beautiful* magazine from where it had been flung on the coffee table and showed me a picture of a warm and welcoming living room in a very upscale farmhouse.

"I love it!" I said.

After all the nonsense Versel had put up with from Chip, she deserved to live in luxury.

Soon Carmela returned with a tray bearing two mugs of coffee, sugar bowl, creamer, and two generous slices of apple crumb coffee cake, topped with a towering layer of cinnamon-laced crumbs.

I'd already had breakfast at home, but I was hungry. After all, I'd hardly eaten anything at dinner last night, if you don't count that slab of chocolate cream pie, and I certainly wasn't going to count it as I'd eaten it standing up over Mario's sink. And everyone knows food eaten standing over a sink has zero calories.

Conversation pretty much came to a standstill as Versel and I inhaled our coffee cake.

"My, that was dee-lish," I said, when I'd scraped the last crumb from my plate.

"Carmela probably should have nuked it to get it a bit warmer," Versel said, "but I agree. Dee-lish."

Reluctantly we abandoned our forks, with twin sighs of satisfaction.

"So what's going on with your investigation?" Versel asked. "Any idea who might have killed Chip?"

I told her about my three major suspects.

She gasped when she heard about Avery's first husband.

"I always wondered why a sophisticated woman like Avery was dating Chip. Anyone could see he was way out of her league. And she certainly didn't need his money. So that explains it: She was out for revenge."

"What about Bree and Denny?"

"I sure hope it's not Bree," she said with a sigh. "I can't stand her, of course, and I'm sure she's fully capable of murder. But if she did it, then Cory would undoubtedly be implicated. Probably as an accessory to homicide. The poor guy has had it so tough all his life, it would break my heart to see him in jail."

"And Denny?"

"I never trusted the man. Way too slick and slimy. I wouldn't put anything past him. And he was beyond furious with Chip that day at the winery."

"So if push came to shove, who'd be your choice?"

"I was going to say Avery, but now I don't know. Any one of them could have done it."

So much for getting clarity from Versel. But on the plus side, I'd gotten that amazing apple crumb coffee cake.

"One thing's for sure," she said. "I know you didn't do it. With any luck, the police will find the killer soon, and your worries will be over."

"That's so sweet," I said, giving her hand a squeeze.

"Well, I hate to break up our coffee klatch," Versel said, "but I've got a Pilates instructor coming over soon. Can you believe it? Me, doing Pilates? I'll be lucky if I last five minutes."

"I'm glad you're doing so well," I said, as she led me to the front door. "You deserve it."

We hugged goodbye, and I headed over to my Corolla. I was just about to get in when I remembered my little fib to Mario about moving to Somalia.

I figured I ought to tell Versel, so she could back up my story in case Mario got in touch with her. The last thing I needed was to face the wrath of F.U. if she learned I'd lied about dumping her precious son.

I started back to the house, but stopped in my tracks when I heard a ruckus coming from inside.

It was Versel, screaming bloody murder at Carmela.

"Why the hell didn't you heat up that coffee cake in the microwave?" she was shrieking. "And how many times have I told you? I like half-and-half in my coffee, not milk! You better shape up, missy, if you expect to keep working here. You certainly were MIA the day they handed out brains!"

Holy mackerel. I couldn't believe this shrieking harridan was good-natured, easygoing Versel. Was it possible that underneath her warm and fuzzy exterior she was every bit as venomous as her brother? Maybe her makeover had nothing to do with staving off grief, but everything to do with celebrating her new life out from under Chip's oppressive thumb. Maybe she'd had her fill of living with him as an indentured servant and had smothered him with a throw pillow to break free at last.

I sprinted back to my car and drove off as fast as I could, Versel's angry outburst ringing in my ears.

Darn it all. I'd been so fond of her.

So it was with heavy heart that I added her name to my growing list of suspects.

Chapter Twenty-seven

I drove home from my unsettling visit with Versel, and had just opened the door to my apartment when Lance came bounding up the front path.

"Fabulous news!" he cried, following me into my living room. "I've been accepted into the Empire Club! In spite of your mortifying appearance as the Barefoot Contessa, I made it! I guess they were bowled over by my charm."

"I thought you said they were a bunch of phonies and that you didn't want to join the club."

"I don't remember saying that. I must have spoken in a moment of madness brought on by the sight of your bunions.

"Isn't it wonderful, Pro?" Lance said, scooping up Prozac from where she'd been napping on one of my cashmere sweaters. "Your beloved Uncle Lance is a member of one of the most exclusive social clubs in town!"

Prozac yawned, unimpressed.

It can't be much of a club if I'm not a member.

Plopping her down on the sofa, Lance turned his attention back to me.

"Even if your performance as European royalty left a lot to be desired, I would've never gotten invited to the soiree in the first place if it hadn't been for the contessa. So I owe you."

"I'll say. Big time."

"How about I treat you to lunch today?"

"Gee, I don't know," I said, thinking of that slab of apple crumb coffee cake I'd inhaled. "I just ate."

"Since when has that stopped you?"

He was right, of course. And a free meal was a free meal. I'd make up for it with a light dinner—maybe some Lean Cuisine with a side of Tater Tots.

"Okay, let's do it!" I said.

"Where do you want to go? You choose the restaurant. And it can't be McDonalds."

"Fatburger?"

Lance sighed, one of his patented Healthy Eater sighs.

"Can we please pick a restaurant where I won't need Roto Rooter to unclog my arteries?"

Then I remembered Sean telling me he was waiting tables at a restaurant in Santa Monica. I struggled to remember the name of the place, but then it came to me: Café Mimi!

"Let's go to Café Mimi in Santa Monica. I've heard they've got some really yummy dishes."

The yummiest, of course, being Sean.

Café Mimi turned out to be a charming bistro, with bentwood chairs, black-and-white floor tiles, and a chalkboard listing the daily specials.

"This place is great!" Lance said as we sat down at a table in the back of the restaurant. "How'd you hear about it?"

I wasn't about to tell Lance about my burgeoning crush on Sean. The last thing I wanted was unasked-for dating advice from a man whose relationships rarely lasted longer than a summer cold.

"I must've read about it on Yelp."

Checking out the menu, I was pleased to see they had

burgers and sandwiches for normal people (aka me) and a bunch of salads for health nuts like Lance. The only thing missing from this perfect setting was Sean. I looked around, but there was no sign of him.

Just my luck he wasn't working that day.

Soon a cute young gal in jeans and a Café Mimi tee came to take our orders.

I opted for the Mimi Burger, medium rare, while Lance got the (yawn) chopped veggie salad.

"And curly fries for two," I added.

"But I don't like curly fries," Lance said.

"No problem. I wasn't planning on sharing."

The minute our waitress left us, Lance started blathering about what was sure to be his glorious new life in the Empire Club, full of gala soirees, networking opportunities, and, of course, Mr. Right.

"Just think," he said, reporting from somewhere on Cloud Nine. "I'll be lounging at the rooftop pool when I lock eyeballs with a bronzed Adonis named Chad or Everett or Gavin, who turns out to have a blinding smile, fab abs, and an MBA from Harvard. He'll ask me if I want to go for a swim and I'll say yes and before we've finished our laps we'll be madly in love, like Romeo and Juliet, but with two Romeos, and a suicide-free happy ending!"

"Yeah, I'm sure that'll happen," I said, practically rolling my eyes.

But Lance, still firmly lodged on Cloud Nine, was immune to my sarcasm.

"And that's just the beginning," he went on yakking, his imagination in overdrive. "A lot of show biz types belong to the club. With any luck, I might even be able to sell my movie idea."

"What movie idea?"

"I came up with it on the ride over to the restaurant

while you were talking about whatever it was you were talking about."

(Just for the record, I'd been telling him about my trials and tribs trying to track down Chip's killer.)

"Anyhow, my movie's all about a charismatic shoe salesman who's secretly a spy for the CIA and has to foil an attempt to assassinate Mother Teresa."

"You realize Mother Teresa's already dead, right?"

"Must you always be such a nitpicker? Okay, so he'll foil an assassination attempt on the Pope. Or, even better, Anna Wintour! *Mission Impossible* meets *The Devil Wears Prada*!"

Oh, brother. This time I didn't even try to hide my eye roll.

While Lance continued yammering about what a hit his movie was sure to be, it was my turn to tune out, starring in my own blockbuster love story about a gal and her curly fries. Which at last showed up at the table, along with my burger and Lance's anemic chopped veggie salad.

I was just about to reach for my first handful of fries when Lance cried, "Hell, no!"

At first I thought maybe they forgot to put his salad dressing on the side (a cardinal sin in Lance-land), but I was wrong.

"It's Kelvin," Lance whispered, "my boss at Neiman's, and some other guys from the Empire Club. They just walked in."

Lance quickly hid his face behind a plexiglass display of Café Mimi specialty drinks.

"I can't possibly let them see The Contessa in elastic-waist pants and Cuckoo for Cocoa Puffs T-shirt."

I'd forgotten I'd been wearing my Cuckoo for Cocoa Puffs tee. Maybe it was a good thing Sean wasn't there, after all.

"Quick," Lance hissed, "go hide in the ladies' room. I'll come and get you when it's safe to come out."

Looking longingly at my curly fries, I grabbed a few for the road and scuttled off down a corridor to the ladies' room at the rear of the restaurant.

A clean freak lathering her hands like she was prepping for surgery looked up from the sink as I entered the room with my curly fries and lobbed me a disapproving glare. I could practically hear her thinking, *What sort of slob eats fries in a ladies' room?*

Eager to escape her glare, I ducked into a stall to eat my fries in peace. I was about to chomp down on my first fry when I heard a woman in the next stall ask, "How's it going?"

"Um, fine," I replied.

"What're you up to?" she asked.

My God, could she possibly know I was eating curly fries?

"Uh, nothing much," I stammered. "Just the usual ladies' room stuff."

"Can I come over?" she asked.

"What?" I replied in disbelief.

Just when I was ready to report her to the ladies' room police, I heard her say, "I'm going to have to call you back. Some idiot in the next stall keeps answering all my questions."

Too embarrassed to face her, I waited until she'd left and I'd scarfed down all my fries before venturing out of the stall.

Now what? I wondered, hoping Lance was figuring out a plan to rescue me. For a while, I stood there, leaning against the Kotex dispenser, checking my emails and trying to read a book on my phone.

But it was hard to concentrate with a steady stream of

ladies tinkling and flushing. Finally I'd had enough. This was ridiculous. Was I supposed to wait here for the Empire guys to finish eating?

I love Lance (most of the time, anyway), but this was asking too much.

I left the ladies' room and made my way down the corridor, peeking out into the dining room, where I saw Lance had joined the Empire Club gang seated at the very front of the restaurant, right next to the entrance.

Drat! I couldn't possibly walk past them without one of them noticing me.

When push came to shove, I couldn't bring myself to stomp on Lance's dream. So with a sigh, I trekked back to the ladies' room, determined to somehow make my escape.

Looking around my Kotex-equipped prison cell, I finally saw it. My ticket to freedom: a window above a diaper-changing table. It was sort of high, and I'd have to climb on the diaper-changing table to get to it.

But it was worth a shot.

Once again, I resumed my position at the Kotex dispenser, pretending to check my phone, waiting for the ladies' room to empty out.

It was so darn frustrating. Just when I thought the coast was clear, someone would come in to take a tinkle. Finally, after what seemed like eons, I got a break. The room was empty.

I pulled out the diaper-changing table and scrambled onto it, praying it wouldn't buckle under my weight.

But luckily, as I would later discover when I looked it up online, diaper-changing tables can hold up to two hundred pounds.

Breathing a sigh of relief when it didn't go crashing out from under me, I tried to open the window. It wasn't easy. Heaven knows when that thing had been opened last.

I was struggling to open it when I heard the ladies' room door squeak open.

"What on earth are you doing up there?"

I turned to see a matronly woman, undoubtedly related to the clean freak I'd met earlier, giving me the stink eye.

"Maintenance, ma'am. I'm here to fix this window. It appears to be stuck."

Thank heavens she seemed to buy my story and entered a stall to do her business. Meanwhile, I continued struggling with the window until finally it opened.

Hurray!

I waited until the matronly gal had washed her hands and left the room.

Then, wasting no time, I started climbing out the window.

I stopped in alarm, however, when I looked down and saw it was quite a drop to the alley below. No way was I about to break my bones jumping from this height. So it was back to Plan "A." I'd forget about escaping via the window and walk out the front of the restaurant, praying Lance's Empire Club buddies wouldn't recognize me.

I started to pull myself back inside the ladies' room, but to my dismay, I couldn't budge, my hips lodged firmly in the window frame. With a sickening jolt in the pit of my stomach, I realized I was stuck.

I'd just have to wait until some gal came in to use the restroom and call for help.

But wouldn't you know? No one showed up. The place was hopping and bopping when I was trying to make my escape, but now when I needed help it was a ghost town.

So I had no choice but to call out:

"Help! I'm stuck!"

At last I heard the ladies' room door open.

"Don't worry, ma'am," I heard a man's voice. "I'll go get a ladder, and we'll get you down."

Soon he was back, setting up a ladder under my tush.

"I brought a stick of butter," he said, "as a lubricant."

I tried to wrench my body around to get a look at him, but that darn window was like a vise. I couldn't move an inch.

Now I heard him climbing up the ladder steps, then felt my hips being slathered with butter. After which, he grabbed me and pulled, my hips popping out of that window like a champagne cork at a wedding.

"Take it slowly," my rescuer said, guiding me down the ladder steps. "We're almost there."

Now that I was out of panic mode, I realized that my rescuer's voice sounded awfully familiar.

Oh, no! It couldn't be. But it was.

I turned to see that the guy who'd yanked my tush from the window was none other than Sean.

I burned with embarrassment. Not only had he seen my fanny up close and personal, he'd had to lubricate my hips with butter to pry me free. And I'd thought my CUCKOO FOR COCOA PUFFS tee was embarrassing.

Clearly, I'd hit a new low on the mortification totem pole.

"Sean!" I cried. "What are you doing here?"

"I work here, remember?"

"But I didn't see you when I came into the restaurant."

"I just started my shift. The more important question is: What were you doing trying to climb out the window? Running out on a bad date?"

"It's a long story, but I have to get out of here and I can't leave through the front door."

"No problem," he said. "You can go out the back door."

Duh. Why hadn't I thought of that? I could've just walked out the back door and saved myself all this misery.

I grabbed my purse, which, in my haste to escape, I'd left hanging from the Kotex dispenser, and followed as Sean let me out the back door to the alley, my face still flaming with embarrassment at the thought of Sean getting such a panoramic view of my tush.

"Thanks so much for your help," I said, unable to look him in the eyes. "I really should be going."

"Wait a minute. Don't go. Not yet," he said. "I was wondering if you're free to get together tomorrow. Maybe go to the beach."

Wait, what?

"You want to go out with me?"

"You bet!" he grinned.

Omigosh. My tush hadn't been a turnoff. On the contrary, Sean was probably one of those delightful men who liked a woman with her "boom boom" in all the right places.

Then he shot me a look that set off a five-alarm fire in my panties.

And before I knew it, I was in his arms, on the receiving end of a smoldering kiss.

When we finally came up for air, I asked, "But what about that woman you were talking to on the phone at Paco's Tacos? The one you called 'hon.'"

"That was my sister. Her babysitter stood her up, and she needed me to come over and watch my niece."

Yippee! I love sisters!

I was about to explain how I'd assumed she was his girl-friend/wife, but never got the chance.

Because he'd already zeroed in for another kiss—his hands firmly planted on my freshly buttered hips.

Chapter Twenty-eight

It took me forty-five minutes of scrubbing to get rid of the butter stains on my treasured CUCKOO FOR COCOA PUFFS tee. When I was done, only one small blob remained. I was actually happy to have it there as a memento of my first kiss with Sean.

I'd just hung my tee to dry when Lance showed up, full of apologies.

"I'm so sorry I left you stranded in the bathroom, hon," he said, sailing into my apartment with a small shopping bag slung over his arm, "but the guys from the Empire Club saw me and invited me to sit with them. I was going to text you, but before I knew it, I got caught up in their conversation. We're planning a weekend trip to Cabo. Doesn't that sound fab?"

"Yeah, just peachy. I'm so glad you were having such a fun lunch, while I was stuck in the john listening to ladies tinkling and flushing."

"I heard some woman got lodged in the bathroom window and they had to suction her out with a power vacuum."

Yikes, how facts got mangled in the rumor mill.

"That wasn't you, was it?" Lance asked.

"Of course not," I lied. "When I realized you weren't

coming to my rescue, I walked out the back door and took an Uber home."

"Let me reimburse you for the Uber ride! I insist!"

"Okay."

"But not right now," he said. "I'm saving up for that weekend in Cabo."

Was he the most irritating guy on the planet, or what?

"But look!" he quickly added, handing me the shopping bag he'd been carrying, eager to appease me. "I had the waitress box up your burger and fries!"

Great. Exactly what was I supposed to do with a cold burger and soggy fries?

As it turned out, I ate them.

And actually, they were pretty darn good. Especially washed down with a scoop (or three) of Chunky Monkey.

I woke up the next morning to a gloriously sunny day. Perfect weather for my beach date with Sean. He'd texted me last night, telling me he'd pick me up at eleven.

Now I asked Alexa to check the humidity in Santa Monica: only 32%.

"Yay! A no-frizz hair day for my date with Sean!" I crowed to Pro, who was hard at work clawing my chest for her breakfast. "You remember Sean, that cute steward from the train?"

An enthusiastic meow.

Do I ever!

"He's taking me for lunch at the beach in Santa Monica. Isn't that exciting?"

Clearly not interested in my dating adventures, she resumed clawing my chest.

Yeah. Great. Whatever. My breakfast isn't going to make itself, you know.

After breakfast and a quick round of Wordle, I stood in

front of my closet picking an outfit for my beach date. I'd just decided on white capris, red tee, and navy flip-flops (I was going for the nautical look) when I heard a knock on my door.

It was only nine o'clock. It couldn't possibly be Sean. And it better not be Lance. In spite of my happy ending kiss with Sean, I was still a little peeved at Lance for abandoning me in Café Mimi's ladies' room.

As it turned out, it was none of the above.

Instead, I opened my front door to see the two detectives who'd interviewed me the day after the murder: Detectives H. Banuelos and his partner, L. LaMott.

From the looks on their faces, I could tell a fresh batch of poop was about to hit my fan.

"Ms. Austen," said Detective Banuelos, "we'd like a word."

I ushered them into my living room where they sat side by side on my sofa.

Always thrilled to show off for visitors, Prozac was soon slithering around their ankles, plastering their polyester pants with cat hair. She'd done this same routine on their first visit, and they looked every bit as irritated now as they did then.

"Can you call off your cat, please?" asked LaMott.

"Pro, stop that," I said, scooping her up in my arms.

She glared at them, affronted.

Just FYI, most people think I'm adorable.

After an indignant meow, she promptly proceeded to fall asleep in my lap.

"We've been fielding quite a few complaints about you, Ms. Austen," Banuelos said, glowering at me from under bushy brows.

"Yes," LaMott chimed in, checking her notepad. "From Cory and Bree Miller, claiming you trespassed on private property at their home, as well as the Hilldale Country Club."

"And from the managing editor at *L.A. Magazine*," said Banuelos, "who claims you were trying to pass yourself off as one of her reporters."

"And finally," LaMott added, "from a Mrs. Helen Hurlbutt across the street who says your cat dug up her prize petunias."

As much as I've tried to stop her, Prozac occasionally manages to streak out of my apartment and wreak havoc on the neighbors' lawns, earning me the title of the block's Least Popular Neighbor.

"But Mrs. Hurlbutt's petunias have nothing to do with Chip's murder," I protested.

"We know," La Mott replied. "But it's still considered property damage. Just be grateful she hasn't pressed charges."

"It's obvious you've been going around, asking questions about Chip Miller's murder," Banuelos said, "conducting an investigation of your own."

"Kinda sorta," I admitted.

"Are you by any chance a licensed private detective?"

"Not exactly."

"Then cut it out!" he snapped.

"But I've discovered so much!"

I started babbling about how Avery overheard Cory arguing with Chip in his cabin; how Denny had gone from losing his job at The Muscle Factory to now practically running the place; and finally, how Chip was responsible for the death of Avery's beloved first husband.

If I was expecting a round of applause for my efforts, I was in for a big disappointment.

"So tell us something we don't already know," said LaMott.

"In case you're not familiar with how things work in

homicides," Banuelos reminded me, "the police do the investigating. And the suspects mind their own beeswax."

My stomach sank.

"So I'm still a suspect?"

"Now more than ever."

Gulp. What the heck was that supposed to mean?

"We have a witness," said LaMott, "who saw you standing outside Chip's cabin the afternoon of the murder."

Dammit! Someone had seen me and thrown me under the bus.

Any one of my fellow travelers could've peeked out their door and spotted me outside Chip's cabin, just as I'd spotted Sean.

"It's true I went to his cabin," I confessed, "to have it out with him about the twenty-five thousand dollars he was charging me to replace his tapestry. But when I got there, I lost my nerve and ran back to my cabin. I never even knocked on his door."

"Duly noted," said LaMott, but I noticed she wasn't writing down this precious piece of testimony in her notepad.

"Really!" I cried. "You've got to believe me!"

"No, we don't have to believe you," Banuelos said, as they got up to go. "It's not part of our job description. Just stop nosing around and leave the investigating to us."

"Absolutely," I promised, fingers firmly crossed behind my back.

No way was I about to abandon my investigation.

"I can't afford to go to jail for murder," I wailed to Pro once they'd left. "Especially now that I've met Sean, my possible future boyfriend and eventual hubby. What am I going to do?"

Prozac lobbed me a reassuring purr.

No worries, hon. I'll keep him warm for you while you're doing time.

Chapter Twenty-nine

Technically the sun was still shining. But a cloud of doom hung over my apartment as I prepped for my date with Sean.

I donned my nautical themed capris and tee, but when I looked in the mirror, all I could see was me in an orange prison jumpsuit.

After slapping on some makeup, I corralled my curls in a scrunchie. I didn't even bother to blow my hair straight, too busy worrying that any future dates with Sean would be in the visitor's room of my local penitentiary.

So there wasn't a whole lot of joie in my vivre when Sean showed up on my doorstep, looking tanned and terrific in cutoffs and a Paco's Tacos tee, the streaks of blond in his sandy hair glinting in the sun.

Even the sight of all that adorableness failed to lift my spirits.

"Hey, Jaine."

And then a miracle happened.

He smiled at me.

And suddenly my cloud of doom went poof into the ether. Just one look at his laugh lines, and the sun was once more shining in my life.

The guy was like Valium in flip-flops.

How foolish I'd been to be worried. The police didn't arrest women in elastic-waist capris. Sooner or later they'd uncover the real killer and I'd be back to Model Citizen status.

"Ready for our day at the beach?" Sean asked, beaming his Valium smile.

"You betcha!" I replied.

"You bringing a bathing suit?"

Was he kidding? I'd rather be seen in an orange prison jumpsuit.

"I'm not really into bathing suits."

"You should be. I think you'd look great in one."

Can you believe it? He'd seen a panoramic view of my tush and thought I'd look good in a bathing suit. I was seriously falling for this guy.

By now, Pro had come prancing into the living room.

"Hi, Prozac," Sean said, scooping her up in his arms. "How's my favorite traveling companion?"

She batted her eyes in full-tilt coquette mode.

Missing you, dollface! Whaddaya say you take me to the beach and let Jaine stay home and nap on the couch?

"That's enough from you, young lady," I said, wrenching her from Sean's arms and depositing her on the sofa, where, after shooting me the filthiest of looks, she began clawing a throw pillow.

"We'd better get out of here," I said to Sean, "before my little drama queen starts chewing the scenery—literally. She's been known to chew her way through a Pringles can to get at the chips."

A proud meow.

It's a gift.

"So long, princess," Sean said, giving her a love scratch she didn't deserve.

Then we slipped out the door, Sean leading me to a sporty white Jeep parked out front.

"Great car!" I said, before realizing how high it was set off the ground. Sean was treated to another bird's-eye view of my tush as I wriggled up onto the passenger seat.

"I left the sunroof open," he said, as he got in beside me. "Hope you don't mind."

"Not at all," I assured him, grateful I hadn't bothered taming my curls. They'd go wild in no time whipping around in the wind.

"And we're off!" he said, starting the engine.

Soon we were en route to the Santa Monica Freeway, the sun warm on my face, sitting practically thigh to thigh with Sean, drinking in the aroma of his citrusy aftershave.

"Thanks so much for rescuing me from Café Mimi's window yesterday."

"My pleasure," he said, with a sexy wink that set my lady parts tingling.

"What were you doing there anyway?" he asked.

I explained how I'd been hiding from the Empire Club gang, trying not to blow my cover as Romanian royalty and keep Lance from getting kicked out of the club.

"You sure are a good friend."

Indeed I was. If only Lance would remember that more often.

"And an imaginative escape artist," he added with another maximally sexy wink.

By now, my lady parts were doing the conga.

"What about you?" I asked, trying to keep my hormones in control. "How's that article you were writing?"

"It's done!" he grinned. "I just sent it off to *The Wall Street Journal* this morning. I do freelance work for them sometimes."

Yikes! I was on a date with a writer from *The Wall Street Journal*. Talk about impressed. I sure hoped he wouldn't ask about my latest writing assignment—a gig I'd just received that morning from Toiletmasters for their Bottoms Up Bidet.

"You've got to tell me when the article comes out so I can read it."

"No worries. I'll probably be stopping strangers on the street to spread the news."

"What's it about?" I asked.

"An exposé on a crooked business guy."

"Sounds exciting."

"From your lips to the Pulitzer Prize committee," he said, steering the Jeep onto the Santa Monica Freeway. He rolled up the windows and sunroof to keep out the deafening roar of traffic and turned on his sound system, Diana Krall crooning softly from the speakers.

"You like Diana Krall?" Sean asked, ever the considerate driver. "I'm a huge fan."

"Me, too!"

Yet another thing we had in common, I thought, along with HGTV reno shows, using our ovens to dry our jeans, and our mutual kale-phobia.

We were talking about our favorite Diana Krall tunes (mine: "A Garden in the Rain," his: "Peel Me a Grape") when Sean, squinting into the sun, asked, "Would you mind getting me my sunglasses? They're in the glove compartment."

"Sure thing."

I reached into the glove compartment and had just pulled out his sunglasses when I noticed a laminated press card with Sean's picture on it. But the name on the card wasn't Sean. It was Carlton. Carlton Dickens.

What the heck was that all about?

And then I remembered the story both Versel and Denny had told me—about Scotty Dickens, Chip's first business partner, the brains behind the operation, who turned a single gym into a thriving chain, only to get tossed out on his ear by Chip.

Was it possible Sean was somehow related to Scotty Dickens?

I looked over and saw Sean watching me.

"Damn," he said. "I forgot I had that in there."

"Who are you?" I asked, holding up the press pass. "Sean or Carlton?"

"Carlton," he confessed with a sigh. "I've been meaning to tell you the truth, but kept putting it off."

"Any relation to Scotty Dickens?"

"You know about my dad?"

"Versel and Denny both told me how badly Chip treated him."

"That's putting it mildly. My dad never recovered after Chip aced him out of the business. He'd poured his whole life into The Muscle Factory and when Chip swept it out from under his feet, he fell apart. Started drinking heavily and died at fifty-nine, a broken man. Chip ruined his life—not to mention my mom's."

His eyes had lost their twinkle, replaced by an icy glaze as he stared somewhere off into the distant past.

"I vowed someday to get revenge. I did my homework on Chip and knew all about the Iron Man Express. I'd heard on the cater waiter grapevine that he was impossible to work for, constantly hiring new staff. So I sussed out the name of the employment agency he used and—after forking over a lot of money for a fake driver's license and social security number—got the job as his steward on the Santa Barbara trip. I couldn't risk using my real name, afraid Chip might realize I was Scotty's son."

His lips, which had been so soft and inviting when we kissed yesterday, were now set in a thin, grim line. And the inside of the Jeep, which had just minutes ago seemed so comforting and cozy, now seemed more than a tad claustrophobic. There was a distinct chill in the air, and it wasn't coming from the A/C.

"So you came on board to kill him," I said.

"Of course not!" Sean/Carlton protested. "I came on board to ruin him, just like he'd ruined my dad. That day when you guys went to Santa Barbara, I let myself into his cabin and hacked into his laptop, hoping to find dirt on Chip. And I found a gold mine—evidence of fraud, extortion, and suspicious bank accounts in the Cayman Islands."

"Is that the story you wrote for *The Wall Street Journal*?"

"Yes," he nodded. "I copied the hard drive onto a memory stick, determined to expose Chip and see him rot in jail. But then, after everyone got back on the train, I realized that in all the excitement of getting the goods on Chip, I'd left the memory stick in his computer.

"So I sneaked back into his cabin to retrieve it. Luckily, he was asleep when I got there. I grabbed the memory stick and ran. That's when you saw me coming out of his cabin. Later, when you asked me about it at Paco's Tacos, I made up an excuse about bringing him fresh towels."

He reached over and put his hand on my arm.

"You've got to believe me, Jaine. I swear I didn't kill him; when I left the cabin, he was alive and snoring."

Everything he said made perfect sense. Then why was I so uneasy? Why did the pressure of his hand on my arm send the wrong kind of chills down my spine?

I told myself I was being ridiculous, sabotaging a potential relationship. Maybe there was some part of me that was afraid of commitment. Maybe that's why I'd been single for so many years. I had to stop this destructive pattern of behavior and open myself up to love.

I'd pretty much convinced myself that Sean/Carlton had been telling me the truth when I noticed we were no longer on the Santa Monica Freeway heading out to the beach, but on the 405, heading to San Diego.

"Why are we on the 405?" I asked, trying to keep the growing panic from my voice. "I thought we were going to Santa Monica."

"Change of plan," Sean/Carlton said, with a cryptic smile. "I've got a special place I want to show you."

For once, his smile failed to comfort me. Instead, it sent a fresh batch of chills down my spine. And that icy look in his eyes wasn't helping much, either.

Omigod. What if his "special place" was an abandoned warehouse where he planned to get rid of me for good?

I'd been right to suspect him! I wasn't a nutcase sabotaging a potential soulmate. I was a savvy part-time, semiprofessional private eye who'd stumbled on the truth.

Sean was the killer. Not content with ruining Chip's reputation, he'd sought the ultimate revenge—murder. And now that I'd discovered what he'd done, he'd decided to get rid of me, too!

By now the Jeep felt like a dungeon and I a prisoner chained to the wall. I had to get out. I couldn't just sit there as Sean/Carlton drove me to my death.

Then, for the second time that day, a miracle happened.

Well, not exactly a miracle. Not on the San Diego Freeway, where it happens all the time.

Traffic came to standstill, cars creeping along bumper to bumper.

I wrenched my arm from Sean's grasp and, with fumbling fingers, unlocked the passenger door. Then I pushed it open to make a break for it. But I'd forgotten how high the Jeep was and came tumbling onto the asphalt below, landing on my knees.

"Jaine, what are you doing?" I heard Sean calling after me as I scrambled to my feet and started skittering across four lanes of traffic. Cars were honking, people giving me the finger, but I didn't care. Risking life and limb, I darted across the lanes, nearly getting mowed down by a speeding motorcycle.

At last, I reached the shoulder of the freeway and ran to an on-ramp we'd just passed, knowing Sean wouldn't be able to back up and follow me.

I raced down the on-ramp, getting wide-eyed stares from the people driving onto the freeway.

"Watch out or you're gonna get yourself killed," one of them warned me.

Don't I know it! I thought, remembering the icy look in Sean/Carlton's eyes.

Back on the streets, I ducked into a nearby gas station and asked for the key to the ladies' room. The not-so-friendly attendant, a petulant teen with a colony of zits on his forehead, refused to give it to me unless I bought something.

"The restrooms are for *paying* customers," he said.

Gritting my teeth, I bought a Kit Kat bar and hurried off to the ladies' room, where I locked myself in and called for an Uber, relieved to see the nearest driver, Akbar, was only three minutes away.

I was leaning against the wall, taking deep breaths, trying to get my heart to stop racing, when I heard a woman banging on the door.

"Can you hurry it up in there?"

"I'll be right out," I assured her.

But when I checked my Uber app, I groaned to see Akbar was now *fifteen* minutes away.

Acck. I couldn't risk going outside in case Sean had gotten off the freeway and was on the lookout for me.

I stayed barricaded in the ladies' room for as long as I could, trying to ignore the now-furious woman banging at the door. It wasn't until she finally threatened to call the attendant that I gave up and unlocked the door.

A frizzy-haired redhead stood with her hands on her hips, glaring at me.

"You've got some nerve!" she said, storming past me into the ladies' room and slamming the door shut.

I mumbled a feeble apology, then turned to face the street.

My heart froze at the sight of a tall guy with Sean's build and sandy-blond hair standing guard at one of the pumps.

Omigod. Sean had tracked me down. He'd figured out where I'd gone, and he'd come to drag me to that abandoned warehouse.

But then he turned around, and I saw it wasn't Sean after all, but another tall, sandy-haired guy.

My imagination was clearly in overdrive.

With trembling knees, I made my way to a nearby dumpster, where I spent the next ten minutes crouched down, waiting for Akbar.

When he finally showed up, I hurled myself into his car, shaking like a leaf as he drove me home.

I was so darn terrified, I could barely finish my Kit Kat bar.

You've Got Mail!

To: Jausten
From: DaddyO
Subject: Disaster!

Disastrous news, Lambchop! My wig just showed up, and they sent the wrong one! Instead of Elvis, they sent me Cher. And the costume party's tonight! Gotta call around and see if I can find an Elvis wig here in Tampa.

Love 'n snuggles from your frantic
Daddy

To: Jausten
From: Shoptillyoudrop
Subject: Crisis Mode

Daddy's in crisis mode. Instead of an Elvis wig, he got a Cher wig by mistake. For a minute, I allowed myself to hope that he'd give up on the whole Elvis thing and go as The Great Gatsby to match my flapper outfit.

But he's determined to go as Elvis. He's on the phone right now calling costume shops, trying to track down a wig.

XOXO,
Mom

To: Jausten
From: DaddyO
Subject: Victory!

Yahoo, Lambchop! I found an Elvis wig. Unfortunately I couldn't find one here in Tampa, but I found a shop in Orlando that has three of them! Off I go. I should be there and back in plenty of time to get ready for the party.

LYM (love you mucho!),
Daddy

To: Jausten
From: Shoptillyoudrop
Subject: Too Bossy

I can't believe it, but Daddy's actually driving all the way to Orlando for an Elvis wig! Lord knows how long it will take him. He refuses to use the car's GPS—he says the GPS lady is "too bossy"—and insists that he has an excellent internal navigation system. Talk about absurd. The man gets lost going to the supermarket. I can only imagine what wrong turns he'll be taking en route to his wig.

Time to try on my flapper dress. At least one of us will be showing up at the costume party in style.

XOXO,
Mom

To: Jausten
From: Shoptillyoudrop
Subject: The Ghost of Laura Ashley

Oh, dear. I just tried on my flapper dress, and thanks to all the fudge I've been eating, I can't zip it up! I have no idea what to do. I can't face the thought of wearing that dreadful Lady Elvis costume to the party tonight—which, as bad luck would have it, fits me perfectly. I'm seriously considering putting a floral sheet over my head, and going as the ghost of Laura Ashley.

Oops. Must run. There's the phone.

XOXO,
Mom

To: Jausten
From: Shoptillyoudrop
Subject: Sad News

Lydia just called with some very sad news. Our beloved centenarian, Mildred Kimble, passed away last night. She was such a lovely, lively lady; it's hard to imagine her gone.

In honor of Mildred, the costume party has been postponed. But it was too late to cancel the caterers, and Edna Lindstrom has already whipped up her marvelous Swedish meatballs, so we're all meeting at the clubhouse to celebrate Mildred's life.

XOXO,
Mom

PS. On the plus side, at least now I won't have to show up in public as Lady Elvis.

To: Jausten
From: Shoptillyoudrop
Subject: No Answer

I tried to reach Daddy on his cell phone to tell him about tonight's change of plans, but he wasn't picking up. Finally, I heard his phone ringing in the den. He forgot to take it with him.

Oh, well. I'll break the news to him about Mildred when he gets home.

To: Jausten
From: Shoptillyoudrop
Subject: Still Not Home!

I should have known this would happen. It's almost six o'clock, and Daddy's still not home! I'll bet he got lost and is probably somewhere in Jacksonville by now. And Mildred's memorial starts in ten minutes! I'll just leave a note for him on the refrigerator to tell him about the change of plans.

XOXO,
Mom

To: Jausten
From: Shoptillyoudrop
Subject: Total Fiasco

Thanks to Daddy, Mildred's memorial service was a total fiasco.

It all started out beautifully, with pictures of Mildred on display and a buffet of cold cuts and Edna's Swedish meatballs.

Hanging on the wall was a replica of the original American flag, with thirteen stars, handsewn by Lydia, a permanent addition to the clubhouse décor in honor of her illustrious ancestor.

Feeling guilty about the weight I've gained, I helped myself to just a few slices of roast beef and the tiniest spoonful of potato salad. Okay, maybe it wasn't so tiny, but at least I managed to avoid the dessert table.

Everyone was sharing memories of Mildred—how she never missed her aqua-aerobics class, how as a centenarian, she was still delivering Meals on Wheels to the "elderly," and how she won first prize in the annual Tampa Vistas golf cart race.

As more people got up to make speeches, I was beginning to get worried about Daddy, afraid that maybe he hadn't gotten lost, but had been in some kind of terrible accident. What if he was sprawled out on a highway, waiting for an ambulance to show up? After a while, I'd worked myself up into quite a tizzy and made a solemn vow that if Daddy were okay, I'd never get irritated with him again.

I was praying for Daddy's safe return when Lydia got up to deliver a eulogy she'd written for Mildred, talking about her kindness, her generosity of spirit, and her rum-soaked fruit-cake strong enough to fell Captain Morgan himself.

"We're all going to miss Mildred," she was saying. "And if there was one thing I could tell her right now, it would be, YOU AIN'T NOTHIN' BUT A HOUND DOG!"

Of course, that last part wasn't Lydia. It was Daddy, who'd just come barging into the memorial service decked out in his Elvis regalia—singing at the top of his lungs.

He clearly hadn't seen my note!

Everyone stared at him, flabbergasted. But did Daddy even notice? Of course not! He was so into being Elvis, he didn't notice a thing, not the pictures of Mildred on display or that no one else was wearing a costume.

He kept on singing "Hound Dog" and swiveling his hips a la Elvis. And then, doing all that swiveling—just as I predicted—he threw out his hip.

Before my horrified eyes, he went careening across the room, straight into Edna Lindstrom's Swedish meatballs, sending meatballs flying onto Lydia's flag—not to mention her "Chanel" suit.

Lydia wanted to call an ambulance, but Daddy insisted he was okay and, after plucking a meatball from his Elvis wig, managed to limp out of the clubhouse. (As it turned out, he didn't throw out his hip; he merely tripped on the hem of Elvis's bell-bottom pants.)

I know I should be furious with him, but I remember the vow I made when I thought his bloody body was sprawled out on the highway, so I've decided to forgive him.

XOXO,
Mom

To: Jausten
From: DaddyO
Subject: Minor Mishap

I suppose Mom's told you about my minor mishap at Mildred Kimble's memorial service.

I'm afraid I got a little lost on my way home from Orlando. I'd decided to use the GPS system, and as usual, that bossy GPS lady led me astray and I wound up in Kissimmee, FL, where I stopped for a hot dog. By the time I got home, I was in such a rush to get dressed, I didn't see the note Mom left me on the refrigerator door, telling me that the costume party had been postponed to hold a memorial for Mildred Kimble.

At any rate, in spite of everyone's grief over losing Mildred, I could tell they were awed when I showed up and did my Elvis impersonation—absolute perfection, if I do say so myself. Until the part where I tripped over the hem of my bellbottoms and landed in Edna Lindstrom's Swedish meatballs, where a few of them left minor stains on a poorly stitched flag Lydia had whipped up in her Betsy Ross frenzy.

Your mom has been surprisingly understanding about the whole thing.

Gotta run. The phone just rang and Mom says it's Uncle John's attorney calling from Boston.

Love 'n snuggles from
Daddy

To: Jausten
From: DaddyO
Subject: Disappointing News

Brace yourself, Lambchop. It turns out we're not related to Elvis, after all. It seems Uncle John liked to buy headshots of famous celebrities and autograph them to himself. My cousin Beth apparently got an "autographed" photo of Marilyn Monroe, with the inscription, *Dearest John, I'll never forget our magical night of passion at the Disneyland Motel*.

Oh, well. I may not be related to Elvis, but I'm still looking forward to getting my DNA results. Who knows what exciting news awaits me?

Love 'n stuff from
Your ever-curious
Daddy

To: Jausten
From: Shoptillyoudrop
Subject: I Knew it All Along!

It turns out Daddy's Uncle John got his jollies forging celebrity autographs. I knew it all along! I wouldn't put anything past a man who'd take out his glass eye and toss it in a bowl of mashed potatoes!

XOXO,
Mom

Chapter Thirty

After Akbar dropped me off, I barricaded myself in my apartment, locking all the windows and propping a dining room chair under the front door.

I called Detectives Banuelos and LaMott, neither of whom picked up, so I left them both long rambling messages about Sean, aka Carlton Dickens, and his compelling motive to kill Chip.

Meanwhile, my phone was blowing up with texts from Sean. Ignoring them all, I blocked his number, then tore off my capris and tee, remembering how excited I'd been when I put them on just a few hours ago. What a fool I'd been to think that I had at long last found love.

Changing into a pair of jammies, I hunkered down in bed with Prozac and a comforting bag of Oreos.

It was time, I told myself sternly, to give up any hope of finding Mr. Right. No more dates from hell. No more thinking I'd met my soulmate, only to discover he was a homicidal maniac. (Sad to say, it's happened more than once.)

From now on, I vowed to myself, the only men in my life would be Ben and Jerry and my good buddy, José Cuervo.

I'd focus on my writing, maybe tackle that Great American Novel I'd been meaning to dash off for ages. At the very least, I'd throw myself heart and soul into my latest assignment from Toiletmasters for their Bottoms Up Bidet.

And I'd start my whole new industrious life as a prolific writer right then and there. All I had to do was hop out of bed and make a beeline for my computer.

But alas, I did not hop out of bed. I stayed nestled under my comforter with Pro at my side. I guess I needed time to recover from that ghastly freeway ride.

I'd start writing tomorrow, for sure.

In the meanwhile, I turned on the TV, hoping to soothe my jagged nerves. I tried to watch HGTV, but couldn't do it, remembering that our love of HGTV was one of the many things Sean and I had in common.

Instead, I flipped over to Turner Classic Movies, where they were playing *The Nun's Story*. There was Audrey Hepburn, looking doe-eyed and fabulous in a nun's habit, doing good in the world.

Maybe that's the path I should be following, living a selfless life, giving to others.

For a while the whole idea seemed awfully appealing— never having to appear in public in a bathing suit, my nun's habit camouflaging my dreaded hip/thigh zone.

I gave the whole convent thing some serious thought, but in the end decided I simply couldn't face life without Oreos on tap 24/7.

Prozac and I spent the rest of the afternoon watching what turned out to be an Audrey Hepburn film festival. Well, I was watching. Prozac was mostly snoring, except during *Roman Holiday*. (She has a thing for Gregory Peck.) Somewhere in the middle of *Sabrina* she woke up and began yowling for her dinner.

So I shuffled off to the kitchen and tossed some Hearty Halibut Innards in her bowl, then phoned in an order for a sausage and mushroom pizza for myself.

When I heard a knock on my front door a half hour later, I suddenly felt nervous. What if it wasn't my pizza? What if it was Sean/Carlton, come to polish me off for good?

Reluctantly, I tiptoed to the door and called out, "Who is it?"

"It's me, Phil."

I breathed a sigh of relief. It was the pizza delivery guy.

(Yes, I'm on a first-name basis with my pizza delivery guy. Isn't everyone?)

Pulling the dining chair out from under the doorknob, I got my pizza from Phil, exchanging pleasantries before bidding each other good night.

Once more, I secured the door with my dining room chair. Then I headed for the bedroom with my pizza and a glass of chardonnay—Pro hot on my heels, eager to scarf down her minimum daily requirement of sausage bits.

After polishing off most of the pizza (with Prozac's help) and the rest of *Sabrina*, I channel-surfed, landing on a documentary about Jane Goodall. For a few minutes I considered following Jane in her noble footsteps, studying chimpanzees in Africa, but ultimately decided pass on the idea, figuring my hair would get way too frizzy in the jungle.

Before long, I drifted off into an uneasy sleep, dreaming I was running for my life in a cornfield, Sean/Carlton showering me with gunfire from a crop duster.

I was jolted awake from this Hitchcockian nightmare the next morning by the sound of my phone ringing.

Secure in the knowledge that I'd blocked Sean, I answered it.

"Hi, Jaine, honey." It was Versel Rush, sounding warm

and friendly, her old sweet self, no hint of the harridan I'd heard shrieking orders at her maid.

"Hope I didn't wake you," she said.

"No," I lied, wondering why Pro hadn't clawed me awake for her breakfast at the crack of dawn. But then I saw her at the foot of my bed, chowing down on the remains of last night's pizza.

"I hate calling you at the last minute, but it's an emergency. We're taking the Iron Man Express to Santa Barbara this morning to scatter Chip's ashes. Cory was supposed to write a eulogy, but he just called to tell me he never made it past the first sentence. None of us feels capable of writing something in such short order. And we can't scatter Chip's ashes without saying something. It just doesn't feel right. Can you please join us on board and whip up a eulogy? It's a one-day trip; we'll be back late this afternoon."

Ugh. The last thing I wanted was to go anywhere near that dratted train.

"We'll be serving lunch on board after the eulogy."

"Okay, sure," I found myself saying.

Would I never learn to resist the lure of free food? Besides, I couldn't say no, not after that ten thousand dollars Versel had paid me, not to mention dropping the charge for repairing Chip's tapestry. I really did owe her one.

"Thanks so much, doll! We're taking off from Union Station at ten o'clock."

It was already 8:30. I'd have to scramble to get there on time.

"Okay," I promised, "see you soon."

At least this time I wouldn't have to bring Prozac and suffer through any bloody Carrier Wars.

As soon as I hung up, I hurried to the bathroom for a quickie shower, then tossed on some skinny jeans and a black blouse. I was gathering my laptop and purse when I was suddenly immobilized by a frightening thought:

What if Sean/Carlton was on board?

Versel said they were serving lunch. What if Sean was the one serving it?

I had to protect myself.

So I spent the next fifteen minutes racing around my apartment, searching for a can of pepper spray my mom had sent me from the Home Shopping Channel.

Finally I found the spray languishing in my gym duffle bag—neither one of which had been touched for years—and shoved it in my purse.

It was already 9:15, and I called for an Uber, unwilling to waste valuable time hunting for a parking space at Union Station. My driver, Tamil, showed up in an impressive four minutes, and I dashed out the door without having time to scarf down my daily cinnamon raisin bagel.

I just hoped they'd be serving snacks in the parlor car.

Tamil dropped me off at Union Station, and it was with no small degree of trepidation that I made my way over to the Iron Man Express, praying Sean wouldn't be there to greet me.

Thank goodness, there was no sign of him as I approached the train.

So I hustled on to the parlor car, where the updated Versel 2.0 was seated in what looked like a black designer dress. The only vestige of the rosy-cheeked gal I'd first met in a floral apron and polyester sweatshirt was the knitting in her lap, which looked like it was going to be either a very long scarf or a very skinny tablecloth.

The rest of the gang was there, too—like Versel, all clad in black.

Cory and Bree were looking remarkably chirpy for such a solemn occasion, Bree's eyes full of glee, which quickly turned sour at the sight of me. I guess she was still ticked off about our little tête-à-tête at the Hilldale Country Club.

Avery was on board, immaculately groomed and suitably mournful, while Cassidy sat on one of the swivel chairs, cross-legged, with her eyes closed. Meditating, no doubt.

I was somewhat surprised to see Denny there, too. After all, he wasn't a member of the family. I figured he was there to convince the world (and especially the cops) that he'd actually liked Chip.

But with no cops on board to monitor his behavior, he was slugging down a Bloody Mary, looking happy as a kid getting ready to meet up with a mall Santa.

I glanced over at the bar, hoping to see a breakfast spread, but it was disappointingly bare of anything except cocktail napkins.

"Jaine!" Versel cried, beaming at the sight of me. "So glad you could make it! Thanks so much for coming to our rescue."

"Not a problem," I lied.

"I thought we'd all take turns sharing pleasant memories of Chip for Jaine to incorporate in her eulogy," Versel said, as I plunked down on one of the swivel chairs.

"Do you want to takes notes, sweetie?" she asked me.

"Good idea," I said, opening my laptop.

"Who wants to go first?" Versel asked. "Cory?"

"Sorry," Cory replied, "no pleasant memories here." Like Denny, he was glugging down a Bloody Mary, which had clearly loosened his tongue. "You want unpleasant? Miserable? Nightmarish? I can talk your ear off."

"Cory doesn't mean that," Bree was quick to interject. "I'm sure he has fond memories of his dad, but he's just too overcome with emotion to remember any. As for me personally," she added, "I'll always remember how warmly Chip greeted me the day we first met."

"I'll say." Cory interjected. "With his hand groping your fanny."

"Cory!" Bree hissed. "Cool it."

When it was Avery's turn, she talked about what a kind, caring, and funny guy Chip had been (obviously referring to some other Chip in another universe). I knew only too well how much Avery had loathed Chip for the part he played in her first husband's death. But Avery pulled off her tribute with aplomb. If I didn't know better, I'd have thought she'd actually cared for him.

"One of the things I admired most about Chip was his generosity, contributing to so many charitable causes."

"For the tax write-offs," Cory muttered.

Bree not so gently elbowed him in the ribs, silently commanding him to shut the heck up.

When Versel roused Cassidy from her meditation (or a nap, it was hard to tell) and asked her to share a memory of her dad, Cassidy told a sweet story about how Chip used to take her and Cory for carousel rides at the Santa Monica Pier.

"He always insisted that his horse came in first," Cory groused.

"Afterward," Cassidy continued, oblivious to Cory's snark, "he'd take us for ice cream."

"He never let me get vanilla," Cory pouted. "Said vanilla was for sissies."

By now, Bree had given up trying to rein in her resentful husband; instead, she was directing her death-ray glares at me.

We wrapped up our stroll down memory lane with Versel's story about how Chip had taken her in after her husband's death and a highly fictional account from Denny about what a swell boss Chip had been.

"So do you think you have enough material for the eulogy?" Versel asked me when Denny had finished reciting his fairy tale.

"Yes," I said, by now eager to get away from Bree's stink eye.

"You can work in any one of the cabins," Versel said. "Thanks again for doing this," she added with a grateful smile.

I got up to leave, but before I made my exit, I asked, as casually as I could, "So are Mario and Sean back on board?"

Please let her say no, please let her say no.

"Yes, they're both here."

Fooey. I rummaged around in my purse for my can of pepper spray, telling myself not to panic. Surely Sean wouldn't try anything here on the train with so many witnesses. And if he did, I'd just blast him with the pepper spray.

Nevertheless, I was more than a tad terrified when I left the parlor car and opened the door to the sleeper car. What if Sean came darting out from one of the cabins, ready to attack?

But the coast remained blissfully clear as I raced to my old cabin and locked the door behind me.

After my heart stopped fibrillating, I opened my laptop to write Chip's eulogy. But I couldn't seem to get started. In a classic work-avoidance move, I began surfing the Internet, checking out my Facebook page, *The New York Times* headlines, and pictures of chocolate eclairs on Pinterest.

So desperate was I to escape the onerous chore ahead, I even checked out the latest missives from my parents, shuddering at the thought of Daddy crash-landing in Edna Lindstrom's Swedish meatballs. But on the bright side, at least he'd let go of his crazy Elvis obsession.

At last, I could avoid it no longer. I had to write that

damn eulogy. I looked over the notes I'd taken in the parlor car and tried to cobble together a few positive paragraphs about Chip. But once again, I was paralyzed, staring at the relentlessly blinking cursor, distracted not only by the memory of yesterday's hair-raising freeway ride, but by the memory of Chip himself and how he'd been so eager to sock me with that twenty-five-thousand-dollar tapestry bill.

Even more distracting, I could now smell Mario cooking a roast chicken in the kitchen. My stomach rumbled with hunger.

Lest you forget, I'd skipped my breakfast CRB, and by now, I was famished.

I tried to concentrate on the eulogy, but all I could think of was that roast chicken. I simply had to have some of it.

Sensible Me told me to stay safe in my cabin and not risk running into Sean. But Hungry Me said, "Go for it, girl! You deserve something yummy to eat."

(She's so much more fun than Sensible Me.)

Armed with my can of pepper spray, I decided to take my chances. Once I'd managed to scarf down some chow, I'd be able knock off the eulogy in no time.

So it was with a growling tummy and can of pepper spray in my pocket that I peeked out my cabin door. Seeing no sign of Sean, I dashed down the corridor and let myself out of the sleeper car. On the platform between the sleeper car and dining car, I peered into the dining room window.

Still no sign of Sean.

For once, lady luck was on my side!

I pulled open the door to the dining room. Now the smell of roast chicken was stronger than ever. My mouth was watering as I dashed through the dining room to the swinging door leading to the kitchen.

It was only when I peeked in the window of the swing-ing door that I saw something that made me come to a screeching halt, all thoughts of chow forgotten.

For there in the kitchen, clenched in a steamy embrace, were Mario and Cassidy.

Wait, what? What were those two doing together? I didn't even know they knew each other. I thought Cassidy al-ready had a boyfriend, the motorcycle dude who'd picked her up from the winery to take her back to L.A.

And wasn't Mario supposed to have the hots for me? Hadn't he told his mother I was his girlfriend?

But clearly, they were an item. Was it possible Mario had been using me as a beard so no one would guess his connection to Cassidy?

(No wonder the guy never made any passes at me!)

I suddenly wondered if this clandestine affair had any-thing to do with Chip's murder.

What if Cassidy was fed up with her bohemian life, liv-ing in that crummy apartment in Venice and selling her paintings at gas stations? What if she'd been every bit as interested in Chip's money as Cory? What if her motor-cycle buddy had driven her, not to L.A., but back here to the train—where she sneaked on board, hid in Mario's room until everyone had retreated to their cabins for their afternoon siestas, then tiptoed over to kill Chip, hopping off the train before it started back to L.A.?

Suddenly I felt an overwhelming conviction that Cas-sidy was the killer.

Yes, I know that just yesterday I thought the same thing about Sean, but this time I was certain I was right.

I had to call the cops.

I spun around and started back to the sleeper car. But I hadn't gone far when I heard the door to the kitchen swing open and turned to see Cassidy coming at me with a ginormous butcher knife. Yikes. That thing was big enough to cut up a cow.

I reached into my pocket for my pepper spray. Thank heavens, I'd remembered to bring it.

By now Cassidy and her machete of a knife were just inches away.

But when I pressed down on the nozzle to blast her with pepper spray, nothing came out. I pressed again. Still nothing.

Damn! The stuff must have dried out sitting in my closet all these years. If only I'd used my duffle bag and gone to the gym more often, I might've noticed an expiration date on the canister.

"I saw you spying on us in the kitchen window," Cassidy said, poking the tip of the knife at my jugular.

"What? No!" I said, desperately trying to tap dance my way out of this mess. "I didn't see anything."

"Cut the bull, Jaine. You were watching me and Mario. And I can't risk anyone finding out about our affair. Otherwise, they might figure out the truth."

"Truth? What truth?" I said, still playing innocent. "I have no idea what you're talking about."

"I think you know exactly what I'm talking about. I googled you and read about all the murders you've solved. I'm sure you've put the pieces together and figured out how I slipped back on the train to kill Chip."

Clutching my arm in a death grip, her knife still at my throat, she began dragging me to the platform between the dining car and the sleeper car.

"Honestly, Cassidy. Your secret is safe with me. I won't breathe a word."

"Damn straight," she said, shoving me outside onto the tiny platform. "You won't be breathing, period."

Outside, the world flashed by, windswept vegetation clinging to rocky cliffs, the Pacific Ocean below us, postcard blue, oblivious to the drama playing out on the Iron Man Express.

"Time to call it a day," Cassidy said, pushing me toward the edge of the platform. "Your choice," she shouted over the wind. "You can jump. Or," she added, brandishing her machete of a knife, "I can stab you to death."

No way was I about to give up so easily.

"You're not going to stab me with that knife," I said with a confidence I didn't remotely feel. "Because if you do, the cops will know it's murder, and they'll be sniffing around, asking questions. And you can't afford to have that happen."

My little mind game seemed to work.

A beat of hesitation as Cassidy considered that I might be right. I took advantage of her momentary lapse to grab her wrist.

Caught off guard, she loosened her grip on the knife, and it clattered to the floor. Before she could get to it, I kicked it out onto the tracks.

Furious, she lunged at me, determined to shove me to my death. Somehow I managed to grab onto a pole at the edge of the platform, clinging to it for dear life, as she tried to pry my fingers loose.

With a sinking sensation, I realized how strong she was. I remembered her prowess in the kayak race, the sheer power of her stroke.

I cried out for help, but my cries were muffled by the wind.

By now, my hands were aching from holding on to the pole; I didn't know how much longer I could last.

"Time to say goodbye, Jaine," Cassidy said, as she felt my grasp weakening.

I couldn't let this happen. I wasn't ready to die. I had places to go, wonders to see, pizzas to eat.

"I knew it was you all along!" I shouted, in a last-ditch effort to save my life. "I told Versel if anything were to happen to me, that you did it."

"Nice try, Jaine," she smirked. "But I'm not buying it. You're a terrible liar."

And suddenly I was filled with rage. If these were going to be my last words, I was determined to hit her where it hurt.

"And you're a terrible painter," I lashed out. "I've seen better art on a ladies' room stall."

This stopped her in her tracks.

"What?" she cried in disbelief.

"And poor Mario. He's boring as hell, but he doesn't deserve to wind up with a homicidal bitch like you."

"Are you kidding?" Cassidy laughed. "You think I really like Mario? I just used him to kill Chip. The minute my inheritance comes through, he's history, and I mean that literally. He knows too damn much."

"Oh, really?" A man's voice had joined in the conversation. I looked over and saw the door to the dining car open. Mario stood there, eyes blazing. "You're going to kill me, too, Cass?"

Cassidy whirled around and saw him, his face rigid with fury.

Caught off guard, she let go of my hand and watched in fear as Mario stepped out onto the platform.

Without thinking, she took a fatal step backward and lost her balance.

Then, like a feather in the wind, she went flying off the platform onto the rocky cliffside.

Her scream of terror pierced the air.

Mario stood there, stone-faced, then started moving toward me.

Omigod, what if he decided to finish what Cassidy started and bump me off?

With every ounce of strength left in my body, I shoved my way past him into the sleeper car.

But someone was blocking my path.

I looked up and saw Sean.

"Jaine!" he said, with what looked like genuine concern. "I thought I heard you screaming. Are you okay?"

Apparently not. Because the next thing I knew, I'd fainted in his arms.

I don't know how long I was out, but when I finally came to, the train had stopped, and Sean was smiling down at me.

"Hello, you," he said. "Had a nice nap?"

"Oh, Sean, I'm so sorry I ever thought you were the killer."

"Is that why you jumped out of my Jeep?"

"Yes," I nodded, ashamed. "When you got off the Santa Monica Freeway, I thought you were taking me to an abandoned warehouse to get rid of me."

"No, I was taking you to Manhattan Beach. I discovered a really cute café called Austen's, and I wanted to surprise you."

"Do I ever feel foolish," I sighed, remembering my frantic dash across four lanes of freeway traffic.

"No, it's all my fault. I should've told you the truth about my dad's connection to Chip that first night when we met up at Paco's Tacos, but I was afraid of losing you."

Lose me? Not a chance.

"Is there anything I can do for you?" he asked, with a smile that sent my hormones racing. "Are you in the mood for what I'm in the mood for?"

"What are you in the mood for?"

"Roast chicken!" he beamed. "It smells great."

He was thinking about food at a time like this??

Yes! Talk about soulmates. Color me in love!

After we'd chowed down on the roast chicken he'd brought from the kitchen, Sean asked, "Anything else I can get you?"

"As a matter of fact, there is."

With that, I reached up and put my arms around his neck.

He needed no further encouragement.

The next thing I knew, he was zeroing in for a kiss.

Wowie zowie. The train may have screeched to a stand-still, but my heart was racing. When we finally came up for air, I said, "You know, I don't think I'll ever get used to calling you Carlton."

"No worries. Everybody calls me Charles."

I blinked in delight.

Charles Dickens and Jaine Austen!

A match made in literary heaven.

Could it be? Had I long last found The One?

Or was this whole thing doomed to be another fiasco in my cavalcade of bad relationships?

Only time (and the next few pages) will tell.

You've Got Mail!

To: Jausten
From: DaddyO
Subject: Worst News Ever!

Just got my DNA results back, and the news couldn't have been worse. Can't bring myself to give you the hideous results. Mom will be writing soon.

Love 'n hugs from
Your devastated
Daddy

To: Jausten
From: Shoptillyoudrop
Subject: Best News Ever!

Guess what, sweetheart? Daddy just got his DNA results back. Of course, the report confirmed that he's in no way related to Elvis Presley. Or Henry VIII. But you'll never guess who *is* his fifth cousin, once removed: Lydia Pinkus!

Isn't that fun? I can't wait to go to the annual Pinkus family reunion.

XOXO,
Mom

To: Jausten
From: DaddyO
Subject: Demanding My Money Back

I suppose Mom told you the revolting news. No way am I related to the Battle-Axe. And no way am I going to the annual Pinkus family reunion. I'm writing the testing service and demanding my money back!

Love 'n stuff
Daddy

To: Jausten
From: Shoptillyoudrop
Subject: Thank Heavens

Thank heavens Daddy has gotten his Elvis fixation out of his system. The worst is over and we can resume life as usual—with the added bonus of having Lydia on our family tree!

XOXO,
Mom

To: Jausten
From: DaddyO
Subject: A Glimmer of Hope

Dearest Lambchop, I was writing a scathing letter to the DNA people when I happened to spot something very interesting on my test results—a relative named H. Ford in Malibu, California. That can be only one person—Harrison Ford! Isn't that thrilling, Lambchop? I'm related to Indiana Jones!

Just picked up a pith helmet and safari suit for the costume party.

Love 'n kisses
Daddy

To: Jausten
From: Shoptillyoudrop
Subject: Raider of the Lost Ark

Now Daddy's convinced he's related to Harrison Ford. He's been going around Tampa Vistas all morning in a pith helmet and safari suit, claiming to be Indiana Jones and looking for a lost ark in the clubhouse canasta room.

Normally, I'd be drowning my frustration in fudge, but not anymore. After my depressing attempt to squeeze into my flapper dress, I've made a solemn vow to stay away from the stuff. Absolutely no more fudge!

Instead I'm trying pralines.

XOXO,
Mom

P.S. They're yummy!

Epilogue

Fans of really bad art will be happy to learn that Cassidy survived her fall and is recuperating in the prison ward of USC General Hospital.

Mario, her accessory to murder, cooperated with the DA's office and was sentenced to three years' probation. He is currently running a taco truck with his nightmare of a mom—a fate, in my humble op, far worse than prison.

As it turned out, Cassidy went to all the trouble of killing Chip for nothing. It seems he left his entire estate to Versel. (So much for "World's Best Dad.")

Sick of all things Iron Man, Versel sold The Muscle Factory to Curves, the women-only gym—and the Iron Man Express to a gazillionaire Arab prince, who uses it to transport his sons' surfboards from L.A. to Santa Barbara.

Out of the goodness of her heart, Versel gave a generous chunk of change to Cory, who promptly lost most of it in the crypto market.

Needless to say, once the money was gone, so was Bree. She divorced Cory for her plastic surgeon, who, as an engagement present, gave her a new pair of boobs.

Meanwhile, Cory has been working with (and dating) Maryanne from membership sales at the Hilldale Country Club.

Avery gave up being a trophy wife and is happily single, running a foundation she funded to improve the lives of construction workers on disability.

Last I heard, Denny was slinging burgers at Denny's.

Not long ago, Versel invited me to lunch, where she confessed that, after three maids quit in less than two weeks, she realized she was becoming every bit as tyrannical as Chip and signed up for anger-management therapy.

Happy with her new self—and her new maid—Versel has more than 100,000 followers on her Instagram page, "Knitting with VD," where she posts pictures of her knitting projects.

And get this: Lance is actually dating a Romanian royal he met at the Empire Club! True, Valentin works there as a busboy, but he's descended from a long line of Romanian aristocrats.

Lance swears it's true love, but Lance finds true love about as often as he gets a spray tan, so I wouldn't bet the rent on it.

As for me, I'm still dating Charles Dickens. Things seem to be going pretty well, but I'm determined not to get my hopes up. Oh, who am I kidding? I'm as giddy as Lance at a sample sale.

When we're not working, Charles and I spend our time watching sunsets at the beach on the Weather Channel, betting which couples on *House Hunters* will be divorced before escrow closes, and taking romantic walks to the refrigerator.

Fingers crossed this thing lasts. I'll keep you posted.

Three Months Later . . .

Mr. and Mrs. Hank Austen
And their grandcat Prozac
Along with Mrs. Emmeline Dickens

Cordially invite you to the wedding of their
daughter, Jaine Abigail Austen, to
Charles Andrew Dickens

Saturday, June third

Sunset ceremony at the beach in
Santa Monica

After-party at Paco's Tacos

After-after party at Ben & Jerry's

One Final Note

The wedding was a dream come true—a glorious ceremony at the beach.

Everyone said I looked radiant.

Life with Charles is all that I hoped for—and more. At long last, I've met the man of my dreams, my soulmate, who brightens my day with his smile, warms my heart with his kindness, and sets my lady parts on fire with his sensual touch.

He calls me his "sweetie pie" and I call him my "lover man."

I've been in heaven, sheer heaven.

And Jaine's pretty happy, too.

XOXO,
Prozac